"For every h... one touch.

Then he leaned back in his chair, deftly dealing the cards. He seemed to have no doubt that she'd accept his challenge. *God, he knew her so well already.*

Zora gazed at him shrewdly. "And what do I get if I win?"

The corners of his mouth tucked into a sexy smile. "You can have a kiss and a touch, too."

Zora chuckled. "That's not what I had in mind."

Tate's gaze slid to her breasts, making her nipples tingle and sending a sluggish heat through her limbs. He reached over the table, rubbing his thumb over her bottom lip. "What *do* you want, then?"

Her brain ceasing to function normally, Zora fought for words, realizing dimly that he was trying to sidetrack her. "Information."

"Anything you want." Tate shrugged, and smirked confidently. "Besides, I'm not the least bit worried. Ready to lay down?"

She fanned her cards out in front of her. "Three of a kind."

Tate's gaze dropped to her mouth and he licked his lips. In that instant, her body tingling, Zora knew that she'd lost.

The question was, was it just the game she'd given away, or her heart, too?

Dear Reader,

Getting It! is the debut book in my debut series entitled CHICKS IN CHARGE. I'm having a ball writing these feisty, headstrong heroines and pairing them up with worthy guys who are able to handle them. (Or so they think.) The idea of a support group created by women for women—where the *chicks* were literally *in charge*—appealed to me, and thus the fictional organization Chicks In Charge was born. (Think Romance Writers of America meets The Sweet Potato Queens.☺) This series will cover the founding board members' stories, and begins with Zora Anderson, the founding president.

Founder of the phenomenally successful organization Chicks in Charge, Zora Anderson has a secret that would ruin her hard-as-nails reputation—her boyfriend flatly refuses to sleep with her. She's hot and bothered and desperately in need of an orgasmic fix. Author Tate Hatcher doesn't know what to think when a woman he doesn't know enters his hotel room—while he's in the shower, no less—then continues to berate him for not seeing to her sexual needs. But one look at her and he's ready to admit fault and rectify his supposed negligent behavior.

Be sure to check out *Getting It Good!*—the next story in the series coming to Harlequin Blaze in February! And be sure to drop by my Web site at www.booksbyRhondaNelson.com. I love to hear from my readers!

Happy reading,

Rhonda Nelson

Books by Rhonda Nelson

HARLEQUIN TEMPTATION	HARLEQUIN BLAZE
973—UNFORGETTABLE	75—JUST TOYING AROUND...
	81—SHOW & TELL
	115—PICTURE ME SEXY
	140—THE SEX DIET
	158—1-900-LOVER

Getting It!
RHONDA NELSON

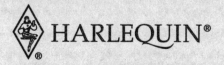

HARLEQUIN®

TORONTO • NEW YORK • LONDON
AMSTERDAM • PARIS • SYDNEY • HAMBURG
STOCKHOLM • ATHENS • TOKYO • MILAN • MADRID
PRAGUE • WARSAW • BUDAPEST • AUCKLAND

This book is dedicated to the *original* Chick-in-Charge, my best friend and critique partner, Debra Webb. Thanks for being the best friend I could ever hope to have, for being a cheerleader, for having enough faith for both of us, for being a drill sergeant, a confidante, counselor, partner in crime, sounding board and all-around bud. I'm proud to be your "Ethel."

ISBN 0-373-69207-2

GETTING IT!

Prologue

AH, THERE'S CARRIE, Zora Anderson thought as she watched her friend weave her way to the back of the pub. She kept her face schooled in a calm mask, but on the inside she literally wilted with relief. The Bitchfest could begin, and she'd never needed to vent more.

She'd had the day from hell, one of the absolute worst in past and recent memory.

"Sorry I'm late." Looking tired but gorgeous as usual, Carrie Robbins slid onto a bar stool and released a beleaguered breath. "Let the Bitchfest begin." She signaled a waitress for a drink, then cast a glance around the small, scarred table. "So, who's going first?"

"It looks like you need to," Frankie Salvaterra said pointedly, and Zora had to agree. Carrie looked particularly harried this evening, as though she needed to share her weekly woes as much as the rest of them did. "What was the holdup tonight?" Frankie asked. She snorted indelicately, pulled a drink from her beer. "Was your hollandaise too runny again?"

April Wilson's eyes twinkled and she aimed the mouth of her longneck bottle at Carrie. "My money's on your noodles. Limp again, right?"

"Not as limp as his dick," Frankie interjected with a grim smirk.

"Ah, but that begs the assumption that he has a dick," Carrie replied archly. "Which he doesn't, remember? We decided after the noodle incident that he was a ball-less, dick-less worm."

Frankie inclined her dark head. "And a pompous bastard to boot."

Zora laughed at the apt description. Carrie was a fabulous chef, one of the best in the area. But being one of the best didn't keep her boss from constantly criticizing her.

Zora cast a glance at each of her friends in turn. As a matter of fact, "pompous bastard" pretty much described almost all of their respective bosses. Except for hers. She no longer had a boss. Or a boyfriend, for that matter, she thought with a bitter smile—she'd lost both when she'd gotten fired today. Zora hid a shuddering breath behind her beer, checked the burgeoning impulse to alternately scream and cry. But she wouldn't do either because conceding so much as a frustrated tear over that faithless, scheming bottom-feeder would punctuate his victory and she simply wouldn't allow it. So long as she didn't cry, he hadn't won and she hadn't been a fool.

From the sounds of things, though, she wasn't the only one who'd had a bad day. Zora had polled the others before Carrie had arrived, and both Frankie and April had given their days a D for dreadful.

Quite frankly, their weekly Bitchfest at the Bald Monkey Pub in New Orleans's French Quarter was typically the high point of her week. Being able to vent her irritation to the tune of low jazz, cold beer, commiserating nods and righteous indignation on her behalf was, in her opinion, better than paying a shrink a couple hundred bucks an hour. The four had met in college, forged instant friendships, and had provided group therapy through every victory and pitfall ever since. Zora had a great family—a couple of older brothers, a mother and father who'd long since retired to sunnier climes—but this group of women had become the sisters she'd longed for, but never had.

Regrettably, there'd been more pitfalls in recent weeks and Zora knew that something simply had to give. Frankie's cynicism had taken a possibly chronic turn, Carrie's effervescent laughter had lost its usual fizz and April's sometimes annoying but always endearing Pollyanna attitude had dimmed considerably. They were on the Bitter Bitch Express traveling at near-sonic speed and, unless something drastically good happened to derail them, Zora feared they were nearing the Point of No Return. They'd become man-hating cat-lovers with too many microwave dinners in the freezer and a handy vibrator in the bedside drawer.

Zora liked men, was allergic to cats and, other than the occasional bag of popcorn, didn't use her microwave. She preferred takeout. As for the vibrator, she enjoyed every aspect of sex—from the anticipation of a kiss to the final sated sigh of post-orgasm and every minute in between—to be fully satisfied by a battery-operated boyfriend. Her lips curled. She couldn't imagine any of her friends being satisfied with that lifestyle either.

A weary grin caught the corner of Carrie's mouth. "No limp noodles or runny hollandaise this time." She gratefully accepted her beer from the waitress. "Does this mean I'm going first?"

Zora nodded and the others chorused their agreement. Usually the person with the worst news got the honors—getting summarily fired and dumped in the same day undoubtedly qualified—but she didn't mind waiting. She'd get her turn. "Let's hear it."

Carrie leaned back in her chair and gave her head a helpless shake. "What I can say? It's just the same old shit. Martin isn't happy unless he's finding fault and—" her voice developed an edge "—he particularly enjoys finding fault with me." She let go a sigh. "Tonight I didn't put enough feta cheese on the bruschetta." She shrugged. "Tomorrow night it'll be something else."

"Son of a bitch."

"Bastard."

"Asshole."

Verbally flaying the boss in question always made them feel better. Zora quirked a brow. "Any news from *Let's Cook, New Orleans?*"

Carrie flashed a sad smile. "Not a word."

Carrie had unwittingly served one of the creative executives behind the nationally syndicated program. The show had been such a hit, one of the major networks had asked the producers to pitch some other ideas and, after meeting Carrie, they'd talked to her about possibly coming on board. In what capacity exactly, nobody knew. Until then, *Chez Martin*—Martin's restaurant—was the best game in town.

Carrie blew out a breath. "Okay, I'm done. Who's going next?"

April raised her hand. "I will. Frankie's hot Italian temper is running in the red zone—" she slid her a wry glance "—so I know she's got something big to share, and Zora's been entirely too quiet, which means she's made the mental move into her 'calm place.'" April cast a significant look around the table. "And we all know what that means."

Despite everything, Zora couldn't help but grin. April had pegged them perfectly. Frankie had a short fuse, literally erupted when she was angry. Zora didn't. When she felt herself slipping into that kind of irritation, she simply shut it down. While Frankie's approach might be more therapeutic, Zora's was much more calculated…and vengeful. She didn't forgive and forget easily, a personality trait that never failed to annoy the hell out of her well-meaning but meddlesome older brothers. They'd disliked Trent instantly, Zora remembered now. That should have been a clue.

April sighed. "At any rate, mine is very trivial and I don't want to follow them. Any objections?" When none were made, she continued. "Something truly horrible has happened and, while I get the feeling it's not as monumental as what everyone else has shared, it's quite…disturbing." Her brow folded into a troubled frown.

Intrigued, Zora arched a brow. "Disturbing as in they-quit-stocking-my-favorite-ice-cream-at-the-market or disturbing as in Dad-came-out-of-the-closet?" April's grievances tended to run the gamut. And, point of fact, her dad hadn't *willingly* come out of the closet—she'd accidentally discovered him there. Her Web-design company had been contracted to build a site for one of the local gay bars and, rather than simply letting the manager send her some photos, April had wanted to get "the feel" of the place. She fully anticipated seeing gay couples and men in drag, but she hadn't anticipated discovering her father was one of them. Needless to say, it had come as a shock.

"Neither." She drew in a long breath and lifted her shoulders in a small shrug. "I've lost my orgasm."

Numb silence, then, "What? How did you lose it? Where did it go?"

Zora bit the inside of her cheek. "You mean you can't—"

April exhaled mightily. "No." She rolled her eyes. "And believe me, I've tried *everything*. It's—" She struggled for words, shook her head. "It's just…gone."

"Well, it can't be gone for good," Frankie told her, clearly appalled at the very idea. Of the four of them, she was the most vocal about sex, about the male and female roles and the old he's-a-stud-she's-a-whore double standard, one of her favorite rants. "You're just with the wrong guy."

She sighed heavily. "Not anymore. Rob cut and run after a couple of weeks of being unable to satisfy me. His fragile ego couldn't take it."

"You're better off," Carrie told her. "I never particularly liked him." Another unspoken rule—guys were liked until they were history, then instantly became pond scum. Solidarity, the glue that held their unique friendship together, Zora thought with a fond smile. Thank God she had their support.

"Me, either," Frankie seconded. She peeled the label from her beer. "His feet were ugly."

April winced reflectively. "Yeah, he did have ugly feet, didn't he?"

Zora had never noticed Rob's feet, but felt compelled to add to the conversation. "They were hideous."

"Well, I'm sure that your, er…condition isn't permanent," Carrie told her.

April grimaced, then took a drink. "I sure as hell hope not. Who's next?"

Frankie and Zora shared a look. "I think Frankie should go next," Zora said. "I don't mind being last."

Frankie pulled a negligent shrug. "Okay. I caught my dad eating a bagel today," she said lightly.

Carrie and April wore blank looks, but Zora knew the other shoe was about to drop.

"What?" Carrie asked, seemingly baffled. "He cheated on Atkins?"

"No," Frankie replied tightly. "He cheated on my *mother*. The bagel was around the bagel girl's *breast*." Her words were surprisingly clipped, considering she'd uttered them venomously from between slightly clenched teeth.

April gasped and Carrie inhaled sharply. "No!"

Frankie smirked, proceeded to shred the label she'd removed from her bottle. "Yes."

Zora knew that there was some animosity between Frankie and her father—Frankie had worked for her dad for years, but didn't seem to garner the same recognition a son probably would. Furthermore, her father's penchant for infidelity wasn't anything new.

"Oh, Frankie, I'm so sorry," April told her. "I know he's your father, but—" She hesitated.

Frankie laughed grimly, gestured wearily. "It's okay. You can say it. He's a bastard."

"He *is!*" Carrie wailed quietly. "What did you do? What did *he* do?"

She pulled another lazy shrug. "I said, 'What? No cream cheese?' and turned around and walked out."

Despite the hell of her own day, Zora giggled.

Couldn't help herself. Now that was classic Frankie. She might have a short fuse, but it didn't prevent her from thinking quick on her feet.

"Honestly," she continued. "What could I do? Like I said, he's a bastard." She smiled grimly. "But that wasn't the worst part."

God, there was more, Zora thought. "What happened?"

"Turns out the bagel girl's a new graduate in need of a better job. So guess which one she got?"

Zora felt her eyes widen. "No," she breathed, aghast. It couldn't be. Frankie's dad couldn't possibly have done that to her.

Frankie smiled grimly and sadness haunted her dark-brown eyes.

"The VP position?" Zora asked, her voice climbing. "Has he lost his mind?"

Frankie snorted. "I imagine he planted it in the bagel girl this afternoon," she said bitterly, then released a pent-up breath and looked up. "At any rate, I'm unemployed. I walked out today and I'm *not* going back."

"Then that makes two of us," Zora told her. "We can look for a job together."

Carrie's eyes bugged, April's jaw dropped and Frankie blinked. "What?"

"Unlike you, however," Zora continued levelly, "I did not quit, but was fired."

"*Fired?*" they shrieked in unison. "For what?"

Zora felt her lips form a brittle smile. "Officially? Insubordination. Unofficially? He's boinking Carla the copy editor."

April gasped. "He's not!"

"Oh, but he is," Zora insisted, comforted by their outrage.

"That scum-sucking bastard," Frankie hissed vehemently. "After all you've done. How could he—but he can't—" Her face reddened with anger. "You helped *make* that magazine! He couldn't have done it without you!"

A balm and the truth, but there was nothing for it. Trent had always been her "boss." It didn't matter that as creative director she'd helped triple circulation, that she'd practically single-handedly turned *Guy Talk* around. The magazine had been struggling on the verge of extinction when she'd come on board and she'd managed to pull it away from the brink and make it thrive. All that mattered was that he had the authority to fire her, and he had.

But he would pay.

Zora didn't know how or when, but at some point in the not-too-distant future *he would pay*.

Carrie shook her head. "This is simply outrageous. I just—I just can't believe it. What are you going to do?"

Zora shrugged, resigned but not defeated. "Look for another job. In the meantime I've got enough in savings to get by for a while. I hate to spend it, but *c'est la vie*. That's what it's there for."

"Zora, I just don't know what to say." April shot her a sympathetic look. "It's... It's surreal. I thought Trent was the genuine article."

A painful lump formed in Zora's throat, but she managed to swallow it before her eyes watered. "So did I."

"There's no such thing," Frankie countered cynically. "See, this is precisely why I've begun to think that all men are pigs. They can't think past their dicks. They're too busy sticking it to the bagel girl or the copy editor." She harrumphed under her breath. "This would have never happened to you—or to me, for that matter—if a chick had been in charge."

Zora readied her mouth to agree, but a strange sort of tingle started in her chest, the kind that preluded creative genius, a brilliant inspired idea.

She stilled and her gaze drifted to Frankie. "Say that again," Zora said faintly.

In the process of lifting her bottle to her mouth, Frankie paused and frowned. "This would have never happened if a chick had been in charge."

If a chick had been in charge...

Frankie was right, Zora thought dimly as her

mind spun with creative adrenaline. Women were
bonders, nurturers, typically faithful and depend-
able. God knew she depended on her little group
for everything from laughter to advice to therapy
of sorts. They all needed the same thing—support. If she'd had a female boss—if they *all* had female bosses—then, with the exception of April,
who owned her own business, none of this would
have happened. They'd all be better off.

"What?" Frankie asked suspiciously. "I know
that look. That's the I've-got-an-idea look." Her
eyes narrowed thoughtfully. "What are you thinking?"

Zora didn't purposely ignore her, but couldn't
focus on anything beyond her current train of
thought. If a *chick* had been *in charge,* she pondered consideringly, liking the way the phrase
sounded, the empowering message it implied. A
chick in charge... An in-charge chick... No, Zora
thought as inspiration struck.

Chicks-in-charge.

"Zora?" Frankie asked again. "What gives?"

Zora smiled. "You just gave me an idea, one
that I think is going to change our lives."

She spent the next three hours outlining her
thoughts, brainstorming with the other three,
who quickly recognized the potential, and by the
time the bartender heralded the last call of the

night, the concept of Chicks-In-Charge—an organized group created *by* women, *for* women—which promoted personal and professional happiness garnered through self-awareness, self-confidence and independence, was born. They would join forces, help each other. There was strength in numbers. They could change things, Zora decided. Knew it. The board was formed, the president elected and each member held a key role. They were on the cusp of something great, something monumental. A new beginning, a better future. Zora could feel it. They all could.

Frankie slid her a look, grinned. "This is *so* going to kick ass."

Mentally exhausted but curiously energized, Zora smiled and hoisted her beer for a toast. The clink of bottles bumping finalized the deal. "To Chicks-In-Charge," she murmured softly and they each echoed the sentiment.

1

One year later...

"I JUST WANT TO GET LAID," Zora muttered angrily as she made her way back to her hotel room. She stabbed the elevator call button and waited impatiently for a car. Honestly, she thought. It wasn't too much to ask. It had been more than a year. *A year,* she silently wailed, since she'd felt the hard, thrilling weight of a man between her thighs.

Disgusted, embarrassed, thwarted, irritated, but most of all unsatisfied, Zora shook her head at her own stupidity. What the hell had she been thinking? Why had she thought it would be a good idea to get involved with a guy who was into abstinence? Had she lost her mind? Clearly she had. Otherwise she wouldn't be prowling the halls of one of New Orleans's most esteemed hotels—at her first ever Chicks-In-Charge conference, no less, a personal coup—in the middle of the night bemoaning her miserable sex life and her failed attempt at seduction.

That part stung.

On the rare occasions Zora had truly applied herself at seduction, she'd always been successful. In truth, she'd never really had to apply herself. She'd smile an intimate smile, put a little extra swing in her hips, crook her finger and that would be it.

Victory.

But not tonight—and not with Dex.

Annoyingly, Dex not only *had* principles, but *adhered* to them. Initially, the idea of being in an "uncluttered" relationship, avoiding the emotional snarls that never ceased to come up between sexual partners, had appealed to her. She'd just come out a bad relationship—one of the worst, in fact—and had needed the perspective.

She'd thought it would be a good thing.

Ha!

She'd thought wrong.

As the days slid into weeks and the weeks crawled into months, sexual tension had eroded her patience and her ever-weakening resolve to abstain. This extended weekend—this conference, in particular—had seemed like the perfect time to celebrate, and she couldn't think of a better way than a few hours of hot, frantic, sweaty sex. She'd wanted a few melting, toe-curling orgasms and room service.

To that end, she'd booked connecting rooms for her and Dex, spent an ungodly amount of money on a see-through scrap of fabric that any right-thinking male should want to tear off of her and had waxed, exfoliated and perfumed all pertinent parts of her body.

For nothing.

Zora growled low in her throat, stepped into the elevator and jabbed the button for her floor. Dex had firmly—oh-so-embarrassingly—resisted her efforts and, to avoid shrieking at him—Zora didn't shriek, scream, wail or whine because doing so meant she'd lost control of her person, which was completely intolerable—she'd decided to take a walk to cool off. To shut down, de-stress and refocus.

Unfortunately, the lengthy walk had only given her more time to think and the more she'd thought about it, the madder she'd become. She hadn't cooled off at all. To the contrary, she was more pissed now than she had been when she left the room. Because, while she hadn't had any form of sexual relief during their relationship, Dex had. She'd taken care of him, and he'd never once—though he had made a few halfhearted at-tempts—reciprocated the gesture.

In other words, she'd made him come and he'd made her crazy.

This was supposed to have been a fantastic long weekend. Just as she'd suspected when the idea of Chicks-In-Charge had first come to her, the organization had been a smashing success, even more so than what she'd originally anticipated. The idea had struck a chord with women all across America—women who needed advice and guidance wanted to join and become members, and women who had something to offer wanted to participate and share their expertise. The group offered support to women from all walks of life, had banded them together with the sort of single-minded tenacity that had quickly thrust them into the national scene.

They'd started with a local chapter and a Web site—designed by April, of course—and an e-zine that Zora herself had headed up. The e-zine, aptly entitled *CHiC*, had been phenomenally successful and plans were already in the works for a glossy format. As the magazine's resident sex-pert—the Carnal Contessa—Frankie would play a significant role in that endeavor.

As word of the Chicks-In-Charge movement spread, local chapters had swiftly moved across America, and had garnered so much attention that several board members had landed guest spots on late-night TV and early morning shows as well. Zora was currently entertaining several book-deal offers. She'd been interested, of course—she'd be insane not to be—but hadn't moved on anything because, frankly, she didn't know when she'd have the time to write. Between the magazine and her Chicks-In-Charge duties, she didn't have so much as a spare minute, much less the time required to undertake writing a book.

But something had happened recently that had made her come to the conclusion that she'd simply have to *make* the time. Some medieval-thinking yahoo with a too-handsome face and a witty turn of phrase—a fellow New Orleans resident, of all things—had recently written the most unflattering, provoking, ill-informed tome on the "bizarre workings of the female mind." The book, entitled *What Women Really Want, Reading Between the Sighs*, had to be one of the most moronic pieces of so-called literature Zora had ever read.

To add insult to injury, ignorant men, believing they were now going to know how to properly "manage" their women, had abandoned their armchairs, lawn mowers, sporting events and bars and had speedily raced to the bookstores to purchase the damned thing, which had promptly catapulted it onto the bestseller list.

It was precisely this sort of prejudice—this testosterone mentality—that Chicks-In-Charge was fighting, and to have it originate here, in her own backyard, felt like a slap in the face. Zora couldn't recall how many times she'd had Tate Hatcher's little pearls of shit—not wisdom because there was nothing *wise* about his idiotic take on the fairer sex—quoted to her, or how many times she'd had to respond to one of his ignorant ideas. In light of Chicks-In-Charge's success and Tate's equally successful book, the media had paired them up as unwitting adversaries. It was provoking, to say the least.

Zora had read the damned book, several times in fact, because one needed to know one's enemy, and she could see where some people might find it entertaining. The author—dubbed "the last true bachelor"—was unquestionably witty, wrote with a wry sort of humor that under ordinary circumstances would appeal to her. A lot, if truth be told. Unfortunately, being insulted *didn't* appeal to her, which negated any positive thought she could form about the book, or even the author for that matter.

The first time she'd read it, she'd kept flipping the book over and staring at his picture on the back of the dust jacket. Marveling at his stupidity, she'd told herself. She'd *marveled* a lot since then—couldn't seem to help herself. Despite the fact that she vehemently disagreed with every idiotic point made in his book, there was something in that picture—about him, specifically—that drew her.

Naturally, she'd rather be roasted alive than admit it.

But she saw humor and intelligence, a little too much confidence in his heavy-lidded aged-whiskey eyes, and there was something equally obstinate and sheepish about the angle of his jaw, the somewhat full curve of his sexy mouth. Zora paused, remembering, then jerked out of her stupor as the elevator doors slid open once more.

Good grief, she mentally chided. She had enough man trouble without romanticizing the literal author of recent misery. To retaliate, she'd personally written an article for Chicks-In-Charge to debunk each and every point of his ignorant, outdated opinions and had even used his book to showcase the continued stupidity of his own sex. In fact, she planned to deliver that very workshop at this conference.

A pity that such idiocy was packaged in such a handsome body though, Zora thought, unable to completely banish his gorgeous image from her mind. A true injustice.

Which reminded her of another injustice—her

unsatisfied sex life. She wouldn't be able to rectify that this weekend as she'd hoped, but she knew how to start.

By getting rid of Dex.

She'd essentially told him it was time to fish or cut bait. He hadn't fished, so she'd cut bait. Though she was heartily annoyed, she couldn't very well blame him. He'd maintained from the beginning of this ill-gotten relationship that he had no intention of spoiling it with sex. That he wanted a "true" relationship devoid of the drama of copulation. She was the one who'd changed her mind, not him, so if anyone was at fault, technically it was her.

Frankie, who'd thought Zora had lost her mind when she'd shared the parameters of her newest relationship, had correctly predicted this end. She should have listened to her, Zora thought now. Dex had seemed manageable—the only kind of man Zora allowed herself to become involved with. She *had* to be in control, had to have the dominant role in every aspect of the relationship, most especially the sexual aspect. A holdover mentality developed as the result of a relatively harmless, but nonetheless terrifying incident that had happened in her early teens.

One of the neighborhood boys—one she'd had the audacity to humiliate by being a better baseball player—had cornered her one afternoon behind the dugout and pinned her to the ground. Though being raped hadn't been a real danger, the sexual menace underlying the act coupled with the horrifying fear of not being able to *get him off her* had marked her in a way that couldn't be seen. For that one blinding moment, she'd been powerless and, after her brothers had dragged the brute off and beat the living hell out of him, she'd vowed she'd never feel that way again. Would never need another person to fight her battles. She'd been grateful, of course, but a secret part of her had envied them that strength, and she'd wanted it for herself. She thought she'd arrived, inasmuch as she was able.

Zora fished her key card from her robe pocket, planted it in the lock and let herself into her room. A glance at the bedside clock told her she'd been gone for more than two hours. A long time to stew, she decided, even by her standards. The idea of delaying the conversation until tomorrow held considerable appeal, but smacked of cowardice, so before she could think better of it, Zora gave the connecting door a hard push—it had a tendency to stick, she'd discovered earlier—and entered Dex's room.

The light from the bedside lamp illuminated the room—the pile of discarded clothes, specifically—and the hum of the shower told her where she'd find him. Zora barely resisted the urge to snort. The bastard had already had a shower this evening, she knew. His hair had still been a little damp when she'd made her move. That he was in there again begged one of two assumptions. He'd either had to wash her unwanted advances from his pure unsullied body...or he was in there whacking off.

Her money was on the latter.

Her irritation renewed, Zora pulled in a deep breath and let it go as she strolled into the bathroom. "Dex, it's Zora. I hate to interrupt you," she said, purposely loading her voice with innuendo, "but I have something to say."

His shadow behind the curtain momentarily stilled, then resumed movement. Ah, the silent treatment. That figured, she thought, the infantile jerk. Oh, well. The sooner she got this over with the better. She'd tell him what she thought, then go take a shower herself. Had to do something to relieve this infernal tension. Had he changed shower gels? Zora wondered absently, as a wholly masculine scent, one she didn't readily associate with him, reached her nostrils.

Zora dropped the commode lid, sat down and sighed heavily. "Look, Dex. Things, uh... Things aren't working out. Being abstinent is obviously a choice and a viable one for you, at that. But, as we discovered tonight, it's not for me. I thought it was, but it's not. I *like* sex. A lot," Zora added meaningfully as her hollow womb echoed the sentiment, "and, frankly, I miss it."

Zora paused, glared at the shower curtain—his unnaturally still form behind it, specifically—waiting for him to reply. He made a muffled noise, one that sounded ominously like a smothered laugh, but if there were any thoughts clanging around that empty head of his, he was evidently disinclined to share them with her. Still pouting, Zora surmised and expelled a quiet sigh of exasperation.

"I realize things might not have been so difficult for you," she said, her voice somewhat tight, "because you at least have had a few orgasms. I, on the other hand, have not. I don't mean to be cruel," she hastened to add, which wasn't altogether true. She hated a selfish lover and he hadn't even been that—he'd been a selfish *non-*lover. "I'm just being honest with you. Like you were honest with me tonight," she said pointedly. "You resented being seduced—or my attempt, rather," she added with a bitter snort. "And I resent being perpetually…unsatisfied. So obviously this isn't going to work. *I'm* horny. *I* want to get laid. And that puts us at cross-purposes because you don't."

She glared at the curtain again, waiting for some sort of response. Honestly, Zora thought, growing increasingly annoyed with his continued silence. Hell, she hadn't expected him to break down and squall, but a tsk of regret, a token apology, would be nice. Hell, anything but this sulky silence.

She let go a perturbed breath, rolled her eyes. "Don't you have *anything* to say?"

She watched him reach forward and cut off the tap. "Actually, yes."

Zora frowned and the fine hairs on her nape prickled. The shower gel, that voice... Something didn't—

The shower curtain sang across the rod as it was pulled back to reveal six and a half feet of hard, muscled, gloriously proportioned male anatomy. "Hand me a towel."

An anatomy that didn't belong to Dex.

Her gaze traveled from a pair of large, masculine feet up long muscular legs, lingered on the impressive, semi-aroused package located between those legs, then moved upward over six-pack abs and a chest that would make any hetero woman or non-hetero man pant and salivate. Rivulets of water streamed over every perfect part, and though it was completely insane, she was hit with the absurd notion to chase each and every one with her tongue. She wanted to lick him all over.

Until she saw his face—then she inhaled sharply and vainly wished for a hole she could fall into.

For the first time in her life Zora found herself in a situation where she didn't have any idea how to proceed. She was hit with the simultaneous urge to sob, wail, laugh, scream and, most disturbingly, *run.* All of which were intolerable, but for the life of her she couldn't make her brain assimilate any sort of a plan. All she could do was stare, mentally agape, at the naked figure before her. *Naked figure,* her mind repeated, and with a startled flash of insight, his request registered and she blindly handed him a towel. To her chagrin, he didn't immediately fasten it around his hips as any decent man would do, but took his time toweling off instead.

Five o'clock shadow shaded an angular jaw and a faint smile curled one of the sexiest mouths she'd ever seen—but it was the eyes that got her. A pair of disturbingly familiar aged-whiskey eyes—eyes she'd recently studied too intently on the back of a book she wouldn't name—stared back at her. Sweet mother of God, Zora thought faintly…it was *Tate Hatcher.*

THE LAST THING TATE HATCHER expected when he stepped into the hotel shower this evening was to be walked in on by a woman, then have that woman criticize him for not seeing to her "needs."

Quite frankly, he'd been criticized for many things over the years—his cynicism, his inability to commit and various other offenses—but *that* had never been a problem.

He'd never been accused of being a lousy lover, and from the sounds of things, this woman had not only gotten involved with a man who was into abstinence—*what kind of a man didn't want to have sex?* Tate wondered incredulously—but had also managed to hook up with one who didn't…service her at all.

It was utterly mind-boggling.

The moment his startled brain recognized that she'd obviously mistaken him for someone else, Tate knew he should have spoken up and put a halt to her breakup speech, but blatant curiosity had kept him from exercising the courtesy. What sort of woman got involved with a guy who didn't want to have sex? Tate had wondered, morbidly intrigued.

In his research and experience, most women controlled men by wielding sexual power over a guy. If she hadn't used the Vagina Vice, just what sort of method had she attempted to employ to keep him in line? It was something to think about, Tate decided—definitely potential book fodder, which would please his agent—but not right now. He calmly toweled the back of his head. He had other things to attend to right now.

Her voice, when she spoke, was faint and thready. "You're not—"

"Dex," Tate finished helpfully. He finished drying his face. "I know." He'd planned to elaborate, but was met with the second major shock of the night. He blinked, certain his eyes had deceived him.

Long, wavy red hair. Light green eyes. Little Dipper freckle pattern over her slim nose. Gorgeous body. And if she opened her mouth, a forked tongue.

Yep, Tate concluded. It was definitely her.

His mystery woman—the *failed* seductress—was none other than Zora Anderson.

He'd recognize the gorgeous redheaded harpy anywhere, Tate thought, still stunned. God knows he spent enough time listening to her tear his book apart over the past few weeks. The success of his book had coincided with the success of her women's support organization—which had put them in the national spotlight together, a situation that had resulted in much irritation and entertainment. Irritation for him, entertainment for others.

In fact, she and her infernal Chicks-In-Charge conference was the reason he was here—research for his next book. What better way to discredit his critics than to observe them in their element?

His agent, Blake Whitaker, had suggested that a wealth of new book material could be found at the infamous first annual Chick conference, and had practically insisted that Tate find some way to attend. With a deadline looming ahead and no clue for the topic of the next book, he was sincerely hoping that creative genius would strike while he was here. It had to, otherwise he was screwed. What on earth had possessed him to sign a two-book deal? Tate wondered for the umpteenth time. Still, it looked like Blake had been right. Their leader had practically landed in his naked lap, and he hadn't even made it out of his room yet.

Tate felt a disbelieving smile spread over his lips and, though he knew it was awful, he had to forcibly quell a hoot of laughter, a triumphant chortle of joy.

The balls-to-the-wall, hard-as-nails she-devil—*the Chicks-In-Charge president herself*—couldn't get her pansy-ass boyfriend to sleep with her.

Now that was a fortuitous bit of information if he'd ever found any.

Evidently, she'd reached the same conclusion. In a nanosecond, the confusion cleared from her pale green eyes and a knowing little smirk drifted

over her distractingly lush mouth. If she was embarrassed—and she most certainly had to be—
her face didn't display even the remotest clue to
what she was feeling.

"You can lose the shit-eating grin," she said.
She stood and crossed her arms over her chest, let
her gaze drift around the steamy room, purposely
looking at anything but him. "I know who you are
and evidently you know who I am. My question
is this—what are you doing here?"

Quick, too, Tate thought, reluctantly impressed. She'd bypassed all the oh-my-God,
what-a-nightmare drama and moved directly into
damage control/stealth mode. "Since you've
wandered into my bathroom," he drawled lazily,
"I'd say I have dibs on that that question." Tate
smiled. "But we already know the answer to one,
eh? I take it *Dex* was the previous occupant of this
room?"

She bit the inside of her cheek before responding. Summoning patience, he suspected. "Yes, he
was."

"And he left without saying goodbye?" Tate
tutted sympathetically. "That has to hurt."

She glared at him. "Actually, it's a relief," she
said tightly. "Would you mind putting that towel
on, please?"

"Then I must have misunderstood the problem," Tate replied with a feigned frown, enjoying himself immensely. He did as she requested, loosely draped the towel around his hips and stepped out of the shower. "I thought relief is what you *hadn't* been getting."

Her lips formed an irritated smile. "Very cute. But you still haven't answered my question. What are *you* doing here?"

Tate shrugged, purposely avoiding the question. "It's a free country. I can do whatever I want to." It was the equivalent of na-na na-na boo-boo, but what the hell. He was still in shock.

She studied him a moment, and Tate got the most uncomfortable feeling that she was somehow peering directly into his brain, prodding his thoughts. He didn't like it. "I am perfectly aware of the fact that this is a free country and you are certainly at will to do whatever you desire. However, as we both know, *that* was not my question. I asked *what* you're doing here."

"I *was* taking a shower…until you sauntered in here and started harping at me about the sex you need but aren't getting."

Her eyes widened and he watched her lose a notch of that formidable control. "Harping? I wasn't harping. I was perfectly civil. Completely calm."

Tate snorted. Actually, she hadn't been harping. She'd been remarkably composed, especially for a woman who hadn't been properly laid in God knows how long. A tragedy, that, Tate thought as his gaze slid over her, confirming what he'd seen on TV—she was gorgeous. He filed the phenomenon away for further consideration. Regardless, he'd managed to get a small rise out of her—a rare feat, he instinctively knew—and wondered just how far he'd have to go to get her to completely lose it. He was perversely interested in finding out.

"Oh, you were definitely harping," Tate insisted. "Like fingernails screeching down a blackboard." He winced, shook his head. "Could be why your boyfriend had a hard time mustering the enthusiasm to—" he gestured meaningfully toward the bedroom "—*you know*. Most guys don't respond well to criticism. You probably gave him a complex."

Her nostrils flared as she dragged in a harsh breath and she seemed to grow a couple of inches right before his very eyes. She cocked her head. "I don't think I've ever seen anyone so adept at changing the subject and avoiding a simple question. You're purposely baiting me—for your sheer amusement, I can only conclude—and I don't appreciate it." She paused. "Furthermore, you don't have to tell me why you're here." She laughed without humor, rolled her eyes. "That's easy enough to deduce. I'd say I've just given you a very juicy tidbit for your next book—or your next interview, I imagine, given the lamentable state of your character."

"My character?" Tate interrupted as her barb found a mark. He felt his eyes widen. "What could you possibly know about my character?"

"Just what I read in your book." Her lips formed the ghost of a smile. "It was quite…enlightening." Her eyes gleamed with humor, punctuating the thought.

Tate had been fully prepared to defend his character, but the thought was derailed by another more intriguing one. He paused. "You've read my book?" What was he talking about? Of course, she'd read his book! How else could she attack every word in it in that incredibly sexy, lazy voice of hers? Tate stifled a groan.

She smiled one of those superior little grins he'd witnessed in countless interviews. The one that had the curiously disturbing effect of making his blood simmer in his veins and speedily race to his groin. "Of course," she told him. "In fact, I'm using it in a workshop this weekend. Pity you aren't a member of the conference. You might have actually learned something."

Tate returned her smirk. "Yes, well. Since I'm

not a *woman*, I'm not eligible to attend your conference." Not a great hook, Tate thought, suddenly inspired, but he might be able to work with it.

"Ah, but that's not going to keep you from lurking, I see."

Tate chewed the corner of his mouth. "Lurking's not prohibited."

"You're right. It's just tacky."

He shrugged, unconcerned. "If you say so."

"I do. And," she said, drawing the word out as she made her way toward the door, "while this has been interesting, Mr. Hatcher, I think I'll return to my room."

"Don't go on my account," Tate told her, curiously reluctant to see her leave. "I could even get dressed if it'd make you feel better."

Her eyes suddenly twinkled with something akin to wistfulness and her gaze inexplicably dropped to where his towel lay anchored around his waist. Tate felt a surge of masculine pleasure at the telling look. "Sorry," she said. "I don't typically fraternize with the enemy."

Tate chuckled. "The enemy, am I?"

"What else could you be?"

His gaze tangled with hers and he lowered his voice. "You'd be surprised. Maybe we could grab a cup of coffee this weekend. I'd love to pick your brain." Among other things. God, was she hot. Naturally he'd noticed. Still…

She paused and smiled, a genuine curve of her ripe mouth. No mockery, no irritation, just humor and the effect was positively glowing, made her more than pretty, more than sexy. It made her *likable.* "I wasn't aware you thought I had one," she said drolly. "You know. Being female and all."

Tate pulled in a shallow breath, let his gaze drift slowly from one end of her body to the other, purposely lingered over the sweet curve of her hip, the gentle swell of her breasts, then finally settled on her face. "Now that's not a mistake I'm likely to make."

He had the pleasure of watching her cheeks flush and though it could just be wishful thinking on his part—though he doubted it—he thought he detected a flash of reciprocated interest.

She stilled, seemed to weigh an idea, then reach a conclusion. "How about coffee in the morning? Seven, in the lounge? I may have a proposition for you."

Tate nodded thoughtfully, instantly intrigued. "I'll be there."

Without another word, Zora turned and left.

A proposition, Tate wondered consideringly. He couldn't imagine what she had up her sleeve—couldn't imagine it would be anything to his advantage—but that didn't mean he couldn't turn it his way.

He grinned, oddly energized by their little exchange. He had a book to write after all.

2

"NO!" FRANKIE HISSED QUIETLY, her eyes widened in apparent shock. She jerked her thumb toward the connecting door. "He's in there? Right now?"

Zora nodded. Despite her obvious embarrassment, she'd given Frankie the abbreviated version of events. She'd left out the fact that, in some cruel twist of fate, she'd been diabolically attracted to the sardonic jerk.

Of all people for her wayward libido to respond to, it *had* to be him.

It was nauseating.

Granted she'd studied his picture a little too keenly, and the pages of his book were dog-eared from too many reads, but she'd chalked those proclivities up to morbid fascination.

She'd confess to a smidge of attraction—hell, he was gorgeous—but seeing him in the flesh—and she'd seen all of it, Zora thought as the image of his naked body zoomed too swiftly into focus. Smooth tanned skin, supple muscle and the finest dusting of dark hair over his impressive pecs… She let go a shuddering breath. Seeing him in the flesh had taken the barest hint of manageable interest and curiosity, and had compounded it into the mother of all attractions.

Zora would like to blame her intense reaction to him on her neglected hormones, but she knew it wasn't true.

The sound of his voice had made her belly tip and roll.

One look into those mysterious, compelling eyes had made her scalp tingle.

Then he'd smiled, and the tops of her thighs had burned, heat had brushed her nipples, and then camped in her sex. Nothing in her past or present experience could compare.

At best it was inconvenient, at worse it was humiliating.

Renewed embarrassment flooded her cheeks as she remembered her monologue. *I like sex. I'm horny. I want to get laid.* Ugh, she mentally whimpered. Keeping her face schooled into the calm mask she usually wore had been monumentally difficult, particularly when she'd desperately wanted to writhe in mortified agony. She would rather have discovered the Pope in that shower— anyone but him.

Fortunately the business side of her brain had

kicked in and she'd realized that doing damage control—for her reputation and, ultimately for Chicks-In-Charge—was more important than dwelling on her embarrassment. She could do that later. Right now she needed to focus on a solution, which was why she'd called Frankie and asked her to come up to her room. Zora had raided the minibar and fixed them both drinks. She'd considered holding this meeting out on the balcony, but then decided against it—who knew who might be listening, she thought with a dark glance at the wall.

"Yes, he's in there, and yes, I wanted to die," Zora told her, heading that conversation off at the pass. "But instead of moaning about my…unfortunate mistake, we need to think about why he's here."

Frankie blinked. "Well, we know why he's here. That's obvious. He's researching his next book." She frowned and Zora detected a flash of pity in her dark gaze. "So Dex just left? Just packed up and took off without another word?"

Ordinarily Frankie didn't have this hard a time focusing, Zora thought, summoning patience. Furthermore, she wasn't accustomed to being pitied. She didn't care for it. "Yes, that's exactly what he did. The best I can figure out—" though she hadn't dwelled on it "—housekeeping did a speedy cleanup and the lock between our rooms is faulty."

Frankie's lips formed a silent "oh." She winced. "Yeah. That's bad."

"I know," Zora replied gravely. "And what's really bad is that Tate Hatcher knows that I couldn't get my boyfriend to sleep with me." God forbid *he* pitied her, Zora thought suddenly. That would be beyond horrible. "But what does that say about *me* and Chicks-In-Charge? Doesn't sound like I'm in charge at all, does it?"

Frankie knocked back the rest of her drink, set her glass aside. "No, it doesn't, and I hate to drag out the old I-told-you-so, but—I told you so," she said in a long, exasperated wail. "Honestly, there were so many things wrong with that whole scenario. *Not have sex?*" She scowled, shook her head. "I don't trust a guy who doesn't like sex. It's…unnatural."

Zora agreed. Particularly now, when she'd been without for more than a year. But after the Trent fiasco, she hadn't been ready, then Dex had come along and he'd seemed like the perfect solution to her problem. He'd been…safe. And, in all honesty, though it might be considered a little arrogant, she'd never thought that if *she'd* decided she wanted to move their relationship onto a more intimate level that *he'd* refuse. She just naturally assumed that if she came around, he'd follow suit. Her lips twisted.

Clearly, she'd overestimated her appeal.

Zora shrugged. "Well, it's a moot point now, and frankly, I've got other worries."

"Yeah, like how you're going to keep him quiet." Frankie tsk-tsked, shot her a look. "That's going to be tricky."

Zora chewed her bottom lip. "Actually, I think I have a solution."

"Oh? What?"

"I'm going to give him carte blanche at the conference, let him wander around, listen in on every workshop, luncheon, panel and conversation." Her eyes narrowed with determination. "I'm going to let him soak up every single word." Hopefully the message would penetrate that thick, arrogant skull of his, Zora thought uncharitably.

Frankie snorted, shifted in her seat. "Sounds to me like you're arming him."

"Or converting him," Zora countered. "Which would be better, wouldn't you agree?"

"If it worked," she said skeptically. "But, personally, I think it's wishful thinking." She paused, sent her a shrewd glance. "I'm sensing more than an altruistic motive here. What do you get in exchange?"

Zora steepled her fingers and placed them beneath her chin. "The Dex incident remains secret." She pulled a negligent shrug. "That's the most damaging thing he's got, and I can't imagine anything he'd learn in the course of the conference that would be worse."

Which was the truth. Everything she'd worked for—everything she'd put into Chicks-In-Charge—would be lost in the media glee and hype of her failed sex life. She'd become a joke, a mockery and the substantial amount of ground that she'd helped gain through and for Chicks-In-Charge would be lost. The message and the good her organization had done would be forgotten, lost to her misfortune. Furthermore, she never claimed to be infallible, but that didn't make her efforts and that of her sex as a whole any less worthy of respect. But would that be taken into consideration? No. She knew it, which meant undoubtedly Tate Hatcher did, too.

Frankie nodded thoughtfully, seemingly mulling it over. "True," she conceded. "Still, he'll need babysitting. You know, just in case. Who's going to do that?"

She'd already thought of that and the very idea made her tummy tremble. However, this was her fault, so she should bear the majority of the responsibility. "Me, primarily, but I thought we could take turns." Zora grinned, quickly moved to the less troubling part of her plan. "I also thought I'd let everyone know about our *special guest* tomorrow during my keynote speech."

A smile slid across Frankie's lips and her eyes twinkled with humor. "That's devious."

Her language, Zora thought. "That's *smart*," she corrected, her brows arching significantly. "They'll roast him." Wear him down with her chicks, then maybe his head would soften enough to absorb a little of their message, she thought. A dual-fold plan.

Frankie grinned. "I like it."

Zora chuckled. "I thought that part of it would appeal to you." It did to her as well. He might be getting what he wanted, but he damned sure wasn't going to like it.

"So what's the plan?"

"I'm meeting him for coffee in the morning. I'll arrange it then."

Frankie quirked a brow. "And if he says no?"

"He's here for research, remember? He won't say no," she predicted confidently. In that regard they were very much alike, she thought. Were the situation reversed, she definitely wouldn't be able to refuse, and it was precisely that shared trait— that wolf-like, untouchable arrogance—she was banking on.

AH, THERE SHE WAS, Tate thought, as he watched Zora stroll confidently toward *his* table. He masked a triumphant smile with a sip of coffee, purposely ignored the rush of excitement that zinged up his spine the moment he'd caught sight of her.

Predictably, she'd tried to beat him downstairs.

Tate grinned. Hell, he knew enough about intimidation tactics to know that the person who arrived last was at a disadvantage, and given the way she and her friend—a sister *chick*, he assumed—had clucked until the wee hours of the morning—plotting his ruin, no doubt—he felt like he was *dis*advantaged enough, thank you very much. He'd had to get up an hour earlier than what he would have liked, but by God, he was first, and the pleasure of watching her eyes widen with that recognition made missing those few extra minutes of shut-eye worthwhile.

Actually, Tate amended, just watching her *walk* made it worthwhile.

Zora Anderson moved with a confident, sinuous sort of grace that was at once mesmerizing and sexy. Shoulders back, head high, a distinctly feminine swing to her hips, one she didn't try to hide with boxy blazers and mannish suits. Instead, he got the distinct impression that she purposely capitalized on her curvy form. That she reveled in it, enjoyed her femininity.

Today she wore a formfitting pale green suit— the shade of new grass, which coincidentally matched her eyes—that buttoned snugly over her ample breasts and made the most of her small waist. Her rich red hair parted on the side and hung in long, wavy flame-like curls over her shoulders and down her slim back. Unlike most people with her coloring, Zora had only a few freckles and still bore the healthy glow of a decent summer tan. Long lashes framed her curiously exotic eyes, neatly complemented high cheekbones. And her mouth… Tate pulled in a shallow breath.

Her mouth was in a class all its own.

Full, lush, ripe and soft. Particularly her bottom lip. It was plump—suckable—and presently painted with a sheer rosy gloss and curled into the faintest mockery of a smile.

Odd that he found that sexy, that he couldn't wait to hear her so-called proposition and that, rather than gleefully reveling in her mortification last night, he'd been alternately preoccupied with wondering why such a vibrant woman had hooked up with a man who purposely chose *not* to have sex—what had happened to make her think that was a good idea? Tate had wondered—

and thinking about swiftly remedying the unfortunate situation for her.

Repeatedly.

I'm horny, she'd said. *I want to get laid.* Powerful words, Tate decided, particularly coming *from her,* out of *that mouth.* They trumped any preconceived notions he'd had about her. She might look like she had it all together—slick as a firehouse pole—but there were some serious issues hidden behind that calm facade, that lazy, unconcerned, superior smile.

Rather than focusing on Chicks-In-Charge as a whole, Tate had decided that he should concentrate his full attention on one—*her.* He'd contacted Blake last night, shared his good fortune, and his agent had agreed. After all, she was their leader. The organization had been her brainchild. He could undoubtedly learn more listening to her than trying to catch snippets of conversation from other members. He'd still lurk, of course, but he intended to spend the majority of his time with her. Self-serving? Manipulative? Yes. But he didn't care. He hadn't been this psyched in... Hell, never.

Luckily, she'd given him the ammunition to enforce her cooperation last night. She could either calmly accept that he wanted to shadow her, or he'd sing like a canary. Actually, he wouldn't do that—honestly, he wasn't the tactless ogre she apparently assumed—and if there was one thing he'd learned since his book had hit the shelves, it was that there were some things that were simply too personal to share with the general public. Tate grimaced. He had secrets of his own.

He stood as she approached and pulled out her chair. She made a grand show of looking at the chair, then at him. Her expression was deliberately—provokingly—astonished.

"You pulled out my chair?" she said, eyes wide. "But I thought that pulling out chairs and opening doors was just one of those antiquated 'expectations' that us lazy females took for granted?"

"I never said that females were lazy," Tate corrected amiably.

Her lips slid into a droll smile. "No, I believe what you implied was that the downfall of our social culture occurred when women began wearing pants."

Actually, it had been his grandfather who'd thought that and, while Tate didn't altogether agree, the comment—like many in his book—never failed to get a rise out of the female population. It had shock value, which had directly impacted his sales. His company and primary career—Hatcher Advertising—hadn't enjoyed a decade of success for nothing. Tate knew how to market and sell just about anything—including himself.

The idea of the book had started out as a joke, one of those brilliant Saturday-night poker game notions when the huah combination of beer and cigars made every guy an authority on women. He'd started the book for entertainment purposes—his own—and then he'd made the mistake of letting a few buddies look at it. They'd suggested that he shop it around via an agent, and the next thing Tate had known, he'd signed a lucrative two-book deal—thus his quest for new material—and had hit the *Times* list.

Frankly, the whole thing had taken on a life of its own, and he seemed powerless the stop it. In fact, the only way he *could* stop it was to write the second damned book, fulfill the contract, and be done. His publisher kept cracking the whip behind his agent, and his agent cracked the whip behind him. It was a vicious cycle and the constant reminder that he was swiftly running out of time. He couldn't wait to get his life back, to get back into his advertising business full-time.

In his small circle of friends, Tate held the dubious honor of being the most adept at managing the opposite sex.

He'd never had a relationship that had lasted

longer than a month, he'd never been tricked into thinking he was in love—in fact, if he hadn't witnessed the rare phenomenon between the grandparents who had raised him, he'd be hopelessly convinced it was a myth—and he'd never permitted a female to direct any capacity of their acquaintance.

In other words, *he* wore the pants.

He'd seen what the so-called awesome power of love could do to people, from both ends of the spectrum. In his parents' case, it had destroyed his father. Hell, who knew about his mother? He hadn't seen her in years.

Though he'd learned about genuine love and respect from his grandparents, he knew they were the exception to the rule, and he had absolutely no intention of letting anyone close enough to see which side of the coin he'd end up with.

It was too damned risky.

Furthermore, he'd never met anyone who'd even remotely tempted him, so keeping his heart and single status up to this point hadn't been difficult. And even if he did, tying the knot was out of the question. The *Times* had gotten it right when they'd dubbed him "the last true bachelor." A lot of things had been printed about him in the maelstrom of his recent success and the majority of it was more fiction than fact. But that—the bachelor comment—had been dead on the money.

Happily married buddies eagerly awaited his downfall, waited for some mystical, mythical female to come along and "tame" him. To grab him by the short hairs and blithely lead him around. Tate felt his lips slide into a grim smile. They'd have a long wait.

No woman—not even this one, he thought as his gaze inexplicably slid to Zora—would get the best of him.

He pushed the chair forward until it hit the backs of her knees, forcing her to sit down. She glared at him over her shoulder.

Tate grinned. "Sorry," he said unrepentantly. "Now what was this proposition you alluded to last night?" he asked, deciding to cut to the chase. Granted, arguing with her would no doubt be entertaining, but he was eager to move ahead to his own proposition. Then he'd be able to argue with her all he wanted.

She set her attaché case aside and turned her coffee cup up so that a waitress could fill it. Her gaze, when it found his, was calm and assessing. "What happened to picking my brain?"

"In time," Tate returned smoothly.

A beat slid into three as she studied him, then said, "That curious, are you?"

Clever girl, Tate thought, reluctantly impressed. A worthy adversary. She knew something was up, knew that sometime between last night and this morning his interest had shifted. "Can't you tell?"

The side of her mouth formed a wry grin. "I daresay I'm a lot more intuitive than the company you normally keep, but that's beside—"

"For clarification purposes," Tate interrupted, "is that comment directed at all of my company, or just that of the female variety?"

"Feel free to interpret it however you wish."

He inclined his head. "Duly noted."

"Now, as to the proposition. You want to gather information for your next book, correct?"

His primary motive, Tate thought, but after last night he was entertaining another agenda as well. He nodded, conceding the point.

"And I want to keep certain aspects of my private life...private."

Tate suppressed a smile. "You mean you don't want me to tell people that Dex wouldn't sleep with you, that even though you'd seen to his needs, he didn't see to yours? That you like sex, you're horny and want to get laid?" Tate secretly thought Dex was a complete idiot, but he had this perverse urge to needle her. To rattle her. To shake that steely reserve.

Her eyes narrowed fractionally and he watched her nostrils flare as she dragged in a silent breath. "In a nutshell, yes."

Tate tsk-tsked. "Yes, I can see where that might be a little embarrassing. Particularly for you, seeing as how you've banded together an entire nation of women under the pretense that you're completely in charge of every aspect of your life, most particularly *men*."

"I have never claimed to be in charge of any man," Zora corrected. "I have merely advocated that women should command respect from the men in their lives, be it a co-worker, son, father, fiancé, husband, boss or boyfriend." He watched her lips form a brittle smile that didn't quite reach her eyes. "There's a difference."

How many of those applied to her, Tate instantly wondered, his senses going on point. There was too much frost in that sultry voice to suggest that she hadn't been burned at least by one or more of those relationships.

In fact, now that he thought about it, she'd always been surprisingly evasive about what had first given her the idea to start her Girl Power movement. She always gave some pat answer about *seeing the need*, then immediately segued into how the idea had been forged over beer at the Bald Monkey Pub, a regular hangout of the founding members. There had to be more to it, Tate decided. Something significant had propelled her—*driven her*—and he suddenly found himself grimly determined to find out what that something was. He had to know. For research purposes, he told himself, justifying his curious quest for information about her.

"So here's what I thought," she said abruptly. "In exchange for keeping my private life private—and just for clarification purposes that means I, personally, as well as individual conference attendees, are exempt from book fodder—you can move freely about the conference and research us to your black little heart's content. Agreed?"

Tate nodded. That seemed fair enough.

She smiled, bent down and retrieved a packet of papers from her case. "Good. I've brought a schedule of events, meal passes, and—" she slid a silver CHiC lapel pin across the table "—an official Chicks-In-Charge pin, which incidentally must be worn in order to be admitted into any conference event."

Tate chuckled, and with a wry twist of his lips, he picked it up. "You expect me to wear this?"

"I insist."

He arched a dubious brow. "Are you really in a position to insist?"

"I believe I am," she said levelly.

A bark of laughter erupted from his throat. This woman had a set of phantom balls if any ever existed. "And why would you believe that?"

She shrugged lazily. "Intuition."

Tate stared at her in brooding fascination, tried to read her. He knew she was bluffing, and yet... "Do you play poker, by any chance?"

One of those rare true smiles caught the corner of her ripe mouth, twinkled to life in that typically shuttered gaze and ultimately hit him directly behind his zipper. "Once a week with the girls," she confided.

"A skilled player?"

She nodded once. "I can hold my own."

He'd just bet she could, Tate thought, once again reluctantly impressed. Honestly, she had to be one of the most interesting, intriguing females he'd ever come across. There was something about her—what, exactly, he couldn't put his finger on—but, despite their obvious differences, he found himself morbidly—unquestionably, unwisely—attracted to her. More so than he'd ever been to another woman, if he were honest.

He could think of a thousand other ways to put that lush mouth to better use and the fact that she could be blunt when it came to what she wanted made her especially appealing. He instinctively knew that she'd be a vocal lover, and he also instinctively knew that she'd want to take the dominant role. How many guys had let her do that? Tate wondered. He mentally snorted. Hell, aside from this moron Dex, how many would have ever complained?

"Are you a poker player as well?" she asked.

"I've been known to play a hand or two," he told her, as his rebellious mind conjured images of her "dominating" him until his eyes rolled back in his head. Sheesh. He had to get a grip. This was Zora Anderson, the woman who had trashed his book at every opportunity, the research inspiration of his *next* book. Being attracted to her was not smart. In fact, it was damned ignorant.

But a foregone conclusion, he knew, and he was man enough to admit it. But he could handle her, dammit, looked forward to it.

"Are *you* a skilled player?" she asked pointedly, throwing the question back at him.

Tate chuckled. "I can hold my own." His gaze tangled with hers and he purposely lowered his voice. "We should play sometime."

She inclined her head and a glint of challenge suddenly sparked in her gaze. Again that flash of reciprocated interest. "I'm game if you are."

"Stakes?"

"To be determined." She paused. "So what do

you say? Can I buy your silence with unlimited access to my conference?"

Tate offered her his hand. "You can."

The moment her fingers brushed his, Tate knew he'd made a tactical error. Her hand was small and soft, and some curious he-man, chest-beating Neanderthal emotion took hold of him. He was hit with the combined urge to defend and protect, to nurture and dominate. The impact jolted him, made every hair on his body stand on end and every bit of the blood in his body speedily race to his groin. His mouth parched, then immediately watered and his shaken gaze instinctively found hers.

She wore a curious expression, one he imagined mirrored his own, and after a stunned couple of seconds, she calmly withdrew her hand. He instantly missed her warmth and the resulting tingle simply touching her had wrought, felt the loss more keenly than he would have ever believed.

"I have your word?" she asked, drawing him back into the conversation. Her voice wasn't quite as steady as it had been a moment ago.

Tate blinked, still shaken. He cleared his throat. "You do, and for the record, it's good."

She gave him an enigmatic little smile. "So I've heard."

Had she researched him? Tate wondered. He'd certainly spent a great deal of time poring over the Internet reading every spare word he could find about her. Had read her damned magazine until he was cross-eyed. But it had never occurred to him that she might have been equally interested. Tate mentally hummed, filed that thought away for—

She stood smoothly, gathered her things. "The conference officially kicks off at noon with lunch. Workshops begin promptly thereafter." She nodded toward the envelope on the table. "It's all in your conference packet. I'm glad we could come to an agreement."

She nodded once, then turned to leave.

"What would you have done if I'd said no?" Tate asked as an afterthought.

She paused and shot him a sexy smile over her shoulder. "It never occurred to me that you'd say no. I bet on your arrogance...and won."

With that parting comment, she turned once more and calmly strolled away. He'd gotten precisely what he wanted—free access to her and her conference, and yet for some reason, he imagined it had something to do with the fact that she'd been the one to suggest it. Tate got the distinct impression that he'd been had. In what capacity, he wasn't sure yet. But he had the grim suspicion he was about to find out.

3

"WELL?" FRANKIE ASKED significantly from the side of her mouth.

Zora managed a benign smile. "He's in here, isn't he?"

In fact, she was hammeringly aware of the fact that he was in the room. Had known before the excited buzz of conversation had alerted her of his presence. Her very bones had hummed with awareness and, as she'd made her way to the front of the room to join the rest of the board, she'd felt his gaze slide like a warm breeze down the length of her body. She'd turned around, caught him in the act and, rather than being embarrassed or even chagrined for ogling her, the beast had had the audacity to smile at her.

Then wink.

She'd been equally annoyed and thrilled at his nerve. Impressed even, because it was exactly the sort of thing she'd do herself. He was purposely trying to unnerve her and, to her horror, she found it was working.

This morning when she'd walked into the lounge and found him waiting for her—when she'd made a point of arriving thirty minutes early to keep that very thing from happening— Zora knew she was in trouble. She'd underestimated him, an unfortunate instance that wouldn't happen again.

Not only was he quick-witted and intelligent...he was *crafty*.

Odd that she should find that sexy, but she did, and in the few hours that had passed since then she'd figured out why. A woman might not like Tate Hatcher's opinions, his ideas, his mode or method of operation—but she never had to wonder about them. He was literally an open book. What you saw was what you got. He was completely, unfailingly, unrepentantly—to the point of being tactless, even—honest.

As far as Zora could tell, the only secret Tate Hatcher had or kept came back to the why/what factor. *Why* was he so mistrustful of the opposite sex? *Why* did he hold such outdated, unflattering opinions of the opposite sex? *Why* had he decided to be "the last true bachelor"? And *what* event or series of events had led the decision?

Zora couldn't imagine, but she knew there had

to be a reason. A person didn't simply lose their trust and faith, didn't typically abhor the idea of marriage and family, for no reason at all. Simply for the sake of it. Something—or more likely some*one*—had made him this way. She wanted to know who, she wanted to know why, and though it was the most ignorant thing she could imagine undertaking, she wanted to "fix" him. Not because she harbored any idea of being the one and only woman to knock him off his glorified bachelor pedestal or any such nonsense—she'd seen too many women walk down that miserable road. No, she wanted to fix him because he was *wrong*.

It was intolerable.

Furthermore, he was a successful, outspoken thorn in her side and if she could bring him around, she would have truly accomplished something. He was a worthy adversary, but he'd be an even more powerful ally. She had a plan for making that happen, one she fully intended to put into motion in just a few minutes.

Zora's gaze inexplicably moved to where he sat across the room. Somehow—and she could only just imagine—he'd managed to ingratiate himself at a table near the front and, from the rapt attention every female at his table was paying him, he'd evidently turned on that considerable charm and done an admirable snow job. Her lips twisted. Let him enjoy the moment, she thought, feeling charitable—she'd apply the salt soon enough.

Regardless, she could dump a truckload on him and the wretch would still be gorgeous. Honestly. Talk about an injustice, Zora thought as a tingle of unwanted heat buzzed her sex. Were there any real justice in the world, he'd have giant incisors and a fur pelt to complement that beastly personality. He wouldn't literally be tall, dark and handsome. Wouldn't have such a sinful-looking mouth, or eyes that made a woman drunk with lust simply by looking into them. He wouldn't have shoulders sculpted out of muscle and an ass that made her palms itch to cop a feel. He wouldn't have sex appeal oozing from every pore, a keen mind and an acidic sense of humor. Her favorite, of course.

Today he wore a trendy yellow-and-white striped shirt tucked into a pair of equally expensive navy-blue trousers. A slimmish gold watch was fastened around his tanned wrist—not one of those clunky weights guys were everlastingly wont to wear—and his hair had that carefully tousled look that was currently in fashion. Untidy, rumpled and sexy as hell. She let go a sigh and her belly fluttered with warmth. She'd like to imagine that he'd spent half an hour in front of the mirror with a tube of hair gel trying to accomplish the look, but she knew better.

He wouldn't invest the time. He had sense enough to know that a good hairstyle wasn't what made him attractive—though it damn sure didn't hurt.

April leaned forward to be heard. "Can you believe this crowd?" she asked, a wide smile on her lips. "This is awesome."

It truly was, Zora thought, eagerly jumping onto a less troubling train of thought. The room was at full capacity, the buzz of excited conversation at fever pitch. Once word of the conference had gotten out, registration had ended up closing within a week. Women from every walk of life were gathered here, all of them with the same goal in mind—to help other women. It was truly astonishing—heartwarming—and she felt a tremendous amount of pride swell in her chest. *She'd* helped do this. It was curiously humbling.

Trent and the resulting experience at *Guy Talk* had been horrible, but she couldn't help but feel that destiny had played a significant part in putting her where she was now. If Trent hadn't been a scheming, faithless bastard, none of this would have happened.

Chicks-In-Charge wouldn't have happened.

The magazine—which she'd staffed solely with women—wouldn't have happened.

Gratifyingly, within a matter of months after she'd left, *Guy Talk*'s distribution had fallen off thirty percent. She'd had the pleasure of watching her own magazine take off while Trent's subsequently nose-dived.

After two months of shitty numbers, he'd called her and begged her to come back. Zora rarely cursed—normally she didn't need to—but in that instance she'd laughed gleefully, then uttered a couple of choice words that had left a shocked, startled silence on the other end of the line. The mere memory made her smile.

The last she'd heard, things had progressively gotten worse and, as a complete stroke of irony, the copy editor who'd unwittingly put the whole ball in motion had recently ditched Trent and *Guy Talk*, and had founded her own chapter of Chicks-In-Charge.

Frankie looked at her watch. "Don't you think we should get started? Time's starting to run short. The first program begins in twenty minutes."

"I'm waiting on Carrie. She should be out in a minute."

Frankie nodded in understanding.

This was too important to start without Carrie,

and she'd done too good a job not to be commended for her efforts. She'd worked tirelessly with the hotel staff to make sure that the catering was pulled off to her exacting standards. Though she'd undoubtedly been in her element and had thrived in her role in Chicks-In-Charge, she'd nonetheless had to put up with a tremendous amount of grief from her boss. Martin was still a demanding, fault-finding asshole and regrettably, though things were still supposedly "in the works," nothing had come of the cable show as of yet. But they all still held out hope.

"Here she comes," Frankie told her needlessly. Zora had already spotted her. The leggy blonde was hard to miss.

Looking harried but happy, Carrie slid into her chair. "You didn't have to wait for me," she admonished quietly.

"I wouldn't have started without you."

A thankful smile curled Carrie's lips and she let go a small sigh. "I appreciate it." She looked around the packed room and her grin brightened. "This is fantastic, guys. It *rocks.*"

It truly did, Zora thought as another wellspring of hopeful pride bubbled through her. Who would have thought a year ago that any of this would have been possible? That their small group of four would have expanded to more than four thousand within six months, then doubled within a year? It was mind-boggling.

Bolstered, Zora pushed her plate away and stood. "It's time," she told them, then made her way to the podium. The moment she stepped up to the mike, the hum of conversation stopped and every eye in the room fell upon her. It was intimidating to say the least, but knowing they all shared a common goal helped take some of the edge off the angst. "Good afternoon," she told them. "I'm Zora An—"

The deafening sound of applause rose, cutting off the rest of her introduction, and she watched in amazement as every person abandoned their chair and stood. They cheered, catcalled, whistled and shouted, and it took every particle of willpower she possessed not to be moved to tears. A lump of emotion formed in her throat and her gaze moved to her friends, all of whom were also on their feet, clapping harder than anyone, their faces wreathed in ecstatic, proud smiles.

"Welcome to the first annual Chicks-In-Charge conference," Zora laughingly called above the din. The noise finally petered out and everyone resumed their seats. "When the idea of Chicks-In-Charge first occurred to me—" she gestured toward her friends "—to *us*—I can honestly say that we never, in our wildest dreams, imagined that it would result in this. That we'd be eight thousand strong and growing. One hundred and eighty four chapters—and growing. It's *phenomenal*." Another round of applause broke out, forcing her to pause. "That tells me that we're fulfilling a need—that each and every one of you who's here has something to offer. This is an organization *of* women *for* women—we have the best interests of our sex at heart—and to that end, this weekend is about equipping ourselves to make better choices, better decisions. Our board— and our conference coordinator, specifically, Frankie Salvaterra—has worked hard to put together a slate of programs that covers everything from money management to do-it-yourself projects to sexual health." Zora smiled as a titter of laughter moved through the crowd. "We've had volunteers from all over the country step forward to chair various subjects, so be sure and let all of these women know how much you appreciate their efforts." Zora grinned and turned to face her friends. "That said, there are a few people whose efforts *I* have appreciated and they all need to be recognized." She gestured toward the table where they all sat. "First, our conference coordinator, Frankie Salvaterra. Frankie, would you please stand," Zora instructed as her friend rolled her eyes and reluctantly got to her feet. "Next is our

Web mistress and conference registrar April Wilson." April stood without being prompted and twinkled her fingers at the room at large. "And last but not least Carrie Robbins, our hotel liaison and chef extraordinaire. If you enjoy your meals, please be sure and thank her. She, just like every member of the board, has worked tirelessly to pull this conference together. Organizing an event of this magnitude takes a lot of patience, a lot of time and a passion for the end result. If you're happy at the end of the conference, please take a moment and let them know."

A zing of anticipation moved through Zora as the final topic of her welcome speech was at hand. Her gaze drifted to Tate Hatcher, lingered long enough to watch apprehension tighten his admittedly gorgeous grin. "Now, one last thing and then we'll adjourn to our programs. You all might have noticed that we have a male among our midst," Zora said drolly. She smiled as a collective murmur of assent and laughter moved through the crowd and every head in the room swiveled to look at Tate. "Considering this is a Chicks-In-Charge conference and we're an all-female group, some of you might be wondering why he's here." Another murmur echoed around the room. "Ordinarily we would have never permitted it, however, this isn't just any guest—*he's special*—and so the rules had to be adjusted accordingly." Zora paused, sent Tate a veiled smirk, then arranged her features into a grave expression. "This man needs our help." She chuckled grimly, rolled her eyes. *"Desperately."* She paused again, could feel the curiosity mounting with every second she waited.

Her gaze sought Tate's once more and a knowing little smile had turned his mouth. He knew what she was about to do—*knew it*—and though he sat there calmly smiling, she knew he wanted to throttle her. Her toes involuntarily curled in her shoes at the thought and a giddy little triumphant laugh tickled the back of her throat.

Zora reached into the podium, snagged the copy of Tate's book that she'd placed there earlier, then held it up for the entire room to see. It had the desired effect. The room gasped and a flurry of whispers started. The women had turned and were eyeing Tate with distrustful curiosity.

"Ah, you've heard about it, I see," Zora sighed knowingly. "From the sounds of things I imagine most of you have read it, too. And those of you who've read it have probably already deduced why this man is here, and why he so very desperately needs our help." She sent Tate a pitying glance. "Our special guest's name is Tate Hatcher and he wrote this book, *What Women*

Really *Want, Reading Between the Sighs.* He's here to research his next book—I don't know what it's called yet—but we thought it would be in our best interests for him to get it *right* this time." Another chuckle moved through the crowd. Zora took a deep breath, prepared to wrap it up and deliver her ultimate blow. "In light of this, I'm giving you a mission, ladies— *educate him.* If you read something in his book that offended you, annoyed you, made you uncomfortable, or was just plain wrong, then let him know. Ignorance is no excuse, and with all of this knowledge of the female mind present, he can't possibly get it wrong again." Zora smiled. "That's it," she told them. "Let's put Chicks-In-Charge!"

Zora turned the mike off and happily— coolly—strode back to her table. A covert glance across the room confirmed that the women were doing precisely as she'd predicted. Tate was currently surrounded by an irritated mob of females, all of them bent with the Chicks-In-Charge mindset, presumably enlightening him to what women really want—*really.* It was all she could do not to howl with laughter.

Frankie nudged her in the shoulder. "I bow to the master," she teased with a shake of her head. "He's going to be miserable."

Zora nodded succinctly, chewed the corner of her mouth to hide a smile. "Good," she murmured. "I love it when a plan comes together."

SHE WAS DIABOLICAL, Tate thought. Completely, thoroughly, without question, the craftiest creature he'd ever had the misfortune to meet.

To his complete astonishment, and evidently the product of a curious flaw in his character, he found this *intensely* sexy. Heat stirred in his loins, his palms itched, his scalp tingled.

Meanwhile, he was mad as hell.

He watched her sidle offstage and join her group of friends—he knew she wanted to dance a little jig, could tell it even from this distance—but she settled for a mere triumphant smile, one that couldn't have been more victorious if she'd had a few yellow feathers accessorizing it.

After their meeting this morning, Tate had known that he'd stepped into some sort of trap—hell, he should have known when she'd given him exactly what he'd wanted that it had been too good to be true—but it had honestly never occurred to him that she'd "out" him to her sister chicks, that she'd essentially throw a handful of scratch at him and instruct them to friggin' peck him to death.

Educate him, my ass, Tate silently seethed. She

was *so* going to pay for this. He didn't know when, he didn't know how. He chuckled grimly, aimed a narrow glare at her retreating back. But he'd get her. He continued to smile, to placate, to pretend to listen as her righteous chicks clucked around him.

Why do you hate women? I bet if you had a wife you'd keep her barefoot and pregnant.

Opening doors is a common courtesy that men of your generation simply don't understand. We're not lazy—you're lazy.

Having bigger muscles doesn't give you a bigger brain. I'd say getting guys to fetch and tote makes us the smarter sex.

On and on and on it went until Tate had to forcibly quell the urge to scream. By sheer force of will he summoned a tight smile. "Ladies, ladies," he said soothingly. "I'll be happy to answer all of your questions, listen to each of your suggestions, but right now I'd like to attend a program." He smiled again. "After all, I, uh...I am here to learn." He almost choked on the words, but they had the desired effect. A few strongly opinionated hens hung around while he gathered his conference packet, but after a moment they, too, took their leave and he breathed a silent sigh of relief.

Honestly, he'd known that his book had stirred

some controversy, had supremely annoyed his female counterparts, but he honestly hadn't had a
clue that he'd seriously pissed off half the population of the damned country. Didn't they realize
it was, for the most part, tongue in cheek? That
he'd taken every old clichéd opinion and exaggerated it in his own dry style?

Given what had just happened, apparently not,
Tate decided.

He'd known the book would appeal to men—
it had all of the master-of-your-domain propa-
ganda that typically appealed every guy—and he
knew it wasn't a particularly flattering book for
women. But women had been writing similar
books on guy hunting, training husbands, coping
with non-committers and whatnot for years, and
Tate had decided that it had been about time for
a guy to be heard. To be the voice of the little man.
And they wanted to cry double standard? How
screwed up was that?

The book was intended to give guys back their
balls for a little while, make 'em laugh, provide a
couple hours of entertainment. The end. He
wasn't trying to change the world or abolish
women's lib. But he had another book to write—
just one more, thank God, Tate silently praised—
and he didn't intend to breach his contract—or

God forbid, backtrack—just because a group of women didn't agree with his exaggerated opinions. They didn't have to. They weren't his target audience. He wasn't writing the book for them.

Or for her, Tate thought as Zora's curvy frame came into view. The same group of women who'd cornered him had surrounded her—presumably letting her know they were up to the challenge of educating him, Tate thought, barely refraining from grinding his teeth.

He waited for them to leave, then moved in. "Well done," he told her, purposely sounding droll. "I didn't see that coming."

Her lips slid into a superior, delighted smile. "I know. That was obvious from the panic-stricken look on your face." She sighed softly. "Would that I'd had a camera," she lamented.

Now see, this was precisely the sort of behavior that had made him write that damned book in the first place. She was gloating, thought she'd gotten the better of him. He simply couldn't stand it. Couldn't stand for her to think for one instant that she'd managed to outmaneuver him. For one blinding instant, the image of his father tipping a bottle back filled his head, caused nausea to well in the back of his throat.

He was in control, dammit.

He called the shots.

He was the unquestionable master of his own damned domain, the captain of his own damned ship.

In short, he was the boss of his world and for whatever reason—be it blessing or bad luck—she'd entered his world, so by default, he was also in control of her. She just didn't know it yet.

But she would.

And he knew the perfect way to bring her to heel—he'd take her to bed. He'd thought of little else since last night when she'd come into his room and accused him of not servicing her properly. She was horny, she wanted to get laid. Fine. He'd lay her. End over end, upside down and sideways if she wanted.

He was utterly fascinated by her, more attracted to her than he'd ever been to another woman. He'd never taken this course of action with another woman before, had never felt this keen, almost obsessive sense of urgency to land between her legs. To bring her around to his way of thinking.

Tate instinctively knew that the only way they were ever going to see eye to eye was if she were flat on her back. His dick jerked behind his zipper at the very idea. *Flame hair, white pillow, creamy skin, suckable mouth.* He wanted to make her lose it. Wanted to watch that too-calm face melt beneath a hard, hot orgasm.

He wanted her.

He could pretend to have some other agenda, then move into seduction mode, but for some reason, he knew she'd appreciate the forthright approach. Furthermore, Tate had enough experience with the opposite sex to deduce when one was attracted to him and, though she might not like it—any more than he did, he imagined—she was every bit as hot for him as he was for her. And she'd been hot to begin with, so tapping that sexual energy should be one hell of a treat. Explosive.

"I think dinner and a few hands of poker are in order tonight," Tate said mildly.

She paused, too quickly reading his mood, and a cautious gleam entered her cool gaze. "Sorry. I have plans."

He smiled benignly. "And now you have more. What time's good for you?"

"Never."

"Never doesn't work for me." He rocked back on his heels, pretended to think about it. "Eight works better."

"Tonight won't work at all—or any night, for that matter. I have conference duties."

"You have to eat."

"Yes, I do," she told him, practically chewing the words, "with the other board members."

Her friends, Tate concluded. Ah, well. They'd understand. He said as much to her and had the privilege of watching a blush—from anger, no doubt—stain her cheeks. "After all," Tate reminded her with a pointed smile. "I'm your *special guest.*"

She sucked in another one of those calming breaths. "Dinner then. No poker. I don't have time."

"Surely you can squeeze in a few hands."

"No," she replied tightly. "I can't."

Tate pulled a thoughtful face. "You know, it's the funniest thing. I can't decide. Are you a chick…or a chicken?"

Checkmate, Tate decided, watching a martial glint spark in those light green eyes. Like him, she couldn't resist a challenge. "Fine," she finally relented. "I'll play. But—"

"Zora!" the dark haired friend—Frankie, if memory served—hissed from the doorway. "They're waiting."

All business once again, she turned and shot him a look. "We'll finish this later." She started toward the exit.

"Right," Tate called after her. "At eight o'clock tonight, remember?"

She heaved a put-upon sigh, strode purposely out of the room. "I'm trying to forget."

"Aw, now that's no way to talk to your *special guest*," Tate needled, purposely goading her, a new favorite pastime.

"Shove it up your special ass."

Tate guffawed, laughed until his sides hurt. There we go, he thought. An unguarded reaction. There had to be more where that came from…and he couldn't wait to find out.

4

———————————

ZORA WAITED UNTIL PRECISELY eight o'clock before she planted the key card into the lock of her door. Actually, she'd been finished with her dinner/meeting with the board more than thirty minutes ago, but she didn't want to give Tate the satisfaction of thinking that she didn't have better things to do than jump when he said so, the insufferable, arrogant jerk.

She'd sat through dinner while her stomach growled, watched her friends rave over their meals and, while she could have gone ahead and eaten with them, then simply had a drink with Tate, she'd decided to wait and order the most expensive entrée on the menu when *he* was picking up the bill. A petty form of revenge, but she didn't care. He'd forced her to go to dinner with him—it would cost him.

One way or another, she thought grimly.

She didn't know precisely what he had in mind—she knew something was brewing in the evil brain of his—but what, exactly, she hadn't been able to discern. Rather than moving from workshop to workshop, he'd shadowed, dogged, *followed* her the whole damned day. Had seemingly hung on to every word, even jotted several notes down. She'd love to get a peek at that notebook, Zora thought, and if the opportunity presented itself, she wasn't above doing a little investigative snooping. She wasn't being nosy or intrusive—she was protecting her assets. Her reputation.

In addition, the smoldering looks he'd been sending her with that intoxicating gaze had made her belly stay hot and muddled, and she'd had the almost irrepressible urge to smile. Odd that, when she desperately wanted to scream.

Specifically, at him.

Zora had never met a man who could so competently irritate her. He made her teeth itch. Made her stomach vibrate, her fingers tremble. She'd felt that heavy gaze on her the entire afternoon and, though it had taken every ounce of her concentration, she'd managed to hang on to her train of thought. She knew he was purposely trying to derail it, purposely goading her for the sheer sport of it. What she didn't understand was why. Why was he so hell-bent on making her lose it? Why did making her crazy seem to be so important to him?

Hell, who knew, and better still, who had time to wonder about it? The conference had kicked off with a bang and to her delight, everyone seemed to be having a wonderful time. So far—other than Tate—there hadn't been any major glitches and things seemed to be moving smoothly. The first slate of workshops had ended with resounding success, the attendees were happy, energized and eager to learn and share with other CHiC members. Other than the continual hum of awareness from, of all places, the perpetual-thorn-in-her-side Tate Hatcher, things would be perfect.

As it was, she couldn't deny that she was attracted to him, couldn't deny that there was a certain charm to his boorish behavior. Ordinarily, arrogance was a turnoff, but for reasons that escaped her immediate understanding, something about Tate Hatcher's "fit," for lack of a better explanation. He was comfortable in his own skin, confident of his intellect and equally confident of his charm. She supposed that made the difference.

By all accounts, she shouldn't like him, and yet…she did. It galled her to no end, but there was no help for it. Just like she couldn't help being attracted to him.

Mercy.

The man was hot, a topic that, to her eternal

frustration, had been discussed at length over dinner. Despite the fact that they all thought his book—and each opinion in his book—was a load of crap, they nonetheless couldn't deny—only bitterly bemoan—the fact that he was gorgeous. Even Frankie, whose standards were particularly high, couldn't come up with a single physical flaw. She'd vowed to keep looking, because according to her, no one was perfect. Frankie had also issued a warning, had told Zora to be careful. As though she didn't know, Zora thought, remembering her friend's shrewd expression.

While Carrie and April hadn't realized that Tate was a potential threat, Frankie had. But then Frankie was more intuitive than most, and had the distrustful nature to go along with it. She'd undoubtedly noted the chemistry between them and, to make matters worse, had heard her tell him to shove it up his special ass. A smile caught her unaware. Giving voice to that thought had come as a complete shock to her. In fact, she hadn't even realized that she'd said it aloud until she'd heard that deep, sexy laugh resonate around the room and consequently follow her down the hall.

Now that he knew he could make her slip up like that, he'd undoubtedly redouble his efforts to get on her nerves, Zora decided. As if he weren't doing a knockout job of that already, she thought with a mental snort. She didn't have a single nerve he hadn't managed to thump and she hadn't even had the *dis*pleasure of his company for a full twenty-four hours yet. To think that another forty-eight loomed ahead made her equally agitated and perversely thrilled.

For some ungodly reason—known only to the Almighty—she *enjoyed* giving tit for tat with him. Looked forward to it, when in truth she should dread the mere idea of his odious company with the sort of horrified revulsion reserved for pelvic exams and root canals. The last thing she should be doing was checking her makeup for flaws, or fluffing her hair, as though his high-handed mandatory dinner was a *date*. Zora gave herself a you-idiot look, then determinedly moved away from the mirror.

She checked her watch. Five minutes past. He was late. That figured, she thought, unreasonably annoyed as something akin to disappointment sprouted in her rebellious breast. She was not disappointed, dammit. She couldn't be, because in order to be disappointed one had to *care* and she didn't. She did not care. She let go a disgusted breath. As a matter of fact, he could rot in—

A knock sounded at the connecting door before she could complete the uncharitable thought, and the tight sensation that had invaded her belly eased marginally, replaced by a secret thrill of anticipation.

Zora schooled her expression into one of indifference and calmly opened the door. "You're late."

"I heard you come in," he offered with a negligent shrug. "I thought I'd give you a few minutes to freshen up. Do your girl thing."

Looking just as handsome as he had the entire day, all six and a half feet of Tate Hatcher strolled into her room and cast an idle glance around. From his vantage point he had a direct view of her bathroom and his smile widened when his gaze landed upon her makeup strewn across the vanity. "Looks like I was right. You're not hiding a friend in there are you?" he asked leaning around to have a better look, the irritating jerk. "Women usually go to the bathroom in pairs, sometimes in packs, I've noticed." He shook his head, sighed as though it were one of the unsolved mysteries of the world. "It's one of those curious anomalies men never understand."

She knew. An entire chapter had been devoted to the subject in his book. "Just like we don't understand why men have the unconquerable need to adjust themselves every few minutes," Zora countered lazily, fervently wishing she hadn't just applied lipstick. Did he have to be so damned perceptive? she wondered.

Tate turned those whiskey-eyes in her direction, and a slow smile dawned on his distractingly perfect lips. Her belly quivered and a current of heat wound through her limbs. "Hell, women are just jealous because they can't pee standing up."

Zora smiled, quirked a pointed brow and held it.

Tate stilled, shot her a skeptical look. "What's that supposed to mean?" he asked warily, gesturing to her expression. "That Sherlock Holmes eyebrow thing?" His eyes widened comically. "You don't mean— No," he scoffed disbelievingly. "You can't…"

Zora continued to smile, enjoying his discomfort. Oh, but she could. Her father had been a big fan of camping. Much to her chagrin, her summer vacations were usually spent *roughing it.* After the second bout of poison oak on her hindquarters, she'd decided that a different method needed to be employed. Furthermore, it had never occurred to her that she couldn't do everything that her older brothers could do—and usually she could do whatever it was better—so why let a little thing like different plumbing stop her? Thankfully, her mother had agreed and had always encouraged her to push the boundaries between the sexes.

It had taken a little while to master the technique, but now she could use a urinal just as easily as a guy could. A curious talent to say the least, but one that came in handy nonetheless.

Zora nodded. "I can," she told him, rocking back slightly on her heels. "Can even write my name in the snow."

For the first time since she'd met him, Tate looked knocked off balance, like he'd been hit between the eyes with an anvil. He wore a faint smile, a disbelieving frown and he seemed to be studying her with fascinated interest, as though she'd just jumped out of one category in that closed little mind of his and landed in another. She rather liked the idea.

"You're not teaching that here are you?" Tate asked, somewhat hesitantly, that smooth baritone a little rusty. "Because that's just…" He scowled adorably. "That's not right."

Zora barely suppressed a laugh. "Not this time. But maybe next year," she added, just to rattle him.

He passed a hand over his face, shot her an unreadable look. "We, uh… We should probably get going."

Zora snagged her purse from the foot of the bed. "Sure."

The upper hand, she thought happily. It was so nice when one held it.

SHE COULD PEE STANDING UP.

Tate had known that Zora Anderson was a special kind of woman—extraordinary, actually. In just the small amount of time he'd spent in her company that had become painfully obvious. She was slick, cool and diabolically intelligent. Fiercely loyal, too, he'd discovered today while following her around. He'd never come across a woman quite like her and to say that he was fascinated by her would be a vast understatement. She was an exotic breed apart, a new species of female to him.

He'd never met a woman who instantly commanded his respect, who instantly attracted him on more than a physical level. There was a cerebral attraction, as well. He wanted in her head as much as he wanted in her panties. A novel experience, to say the least. In fact, though he knew it was shallow, he couldn't recall ever being romantically interested in a woman for her brain. Had never once been turned on by *intelligence*. A nice ass, maybe. A pair of long legs. But a brain?

Never.

Tate wanted to know her thoughts, learn her secrets, taste that plump bottom lip and know the feel of her breast in his palm. He wanted to lick the side of her neck, sigh into the sweet shell of her ear and feel her quiver. He wanted to talk to her about current events—politics, religion, all the taboo subjects guaranteed to result in a heated debate. He wanted to talk about her business, her secret thoughts, her greatest wishes and hidden fears. He wanted to learn every curve and indentation of her body, slide into the hot valley between her thighs and stay there until she screamed his name.

He wanted to *know* her in every sense of the word.

Probably not the smartest endeavor considering that she had the rare distinction of being able to provoke him past rational thinking.

Take today, for instance. One would have thought that siccing her chicks on him during her welcome speech would have been enough torture for any right-thinking, bloodthirsty female—would have been enough punishment for any presumed crime.

But not for Zora.

No, in addition to that sneaky, vindictive little volley, she'd taken every opportunity she could to irritate him. Instead of letting him calmly sit in the back and study her, she'd called attention to him in every workshop, had insisted that he move to the front of the room—his head was too thick to absorb intelligence from the back row, according to her—and had taken every opportunity she could to zing him with her acidic wit.

It was a funny feeling to be simultaneously mad and horny. Tate stayed perpetually confused, couldn't decide what he wanted to do most—kiss that superior smirk off her beautiful face, or throttle her.

Right now, Tate thought as his moody gaze drifted across the table where she sat, kissing her held the most appeal. Rather than eating in the hotel—what she'd wanted, of course, because it would have been easier for her to have her friends arrange a "distraction"—Tate had insisted that they leave and find their fare somewhere else. He'd chosen Mama MoJo's, a cool little Cajun café located on the edge of the French Quarter.

Zora set her menu aside and looked up. "I think I'll have the crawfish-stuffed filet."

She looked entirely too pleased with herself, which told him she'd undoubtedly—deliberately—chosen the most expensive dish on the menu. He barely suppressed a smile, continued to study the entrée selections, though he'd already decided on the chicken and sausage jambalaya. "I haven't had that before, but I'm sure it's good," he commented mildly.

"You should get it, too, then," she suggested sweetly, a sly attempt to max out the bill.

Tate chewed the inside of his cheek to prevent a grin. "Not this time, I think. I'm in the mood for jambalaya. Something a little spicy." Like her. But he'd sample that later tonight when he upped the ante during their poker game. He had a different set of stakes in mind, ones that should appeal to her…competitive nature.

Once their order had been taken, Tate sat back and studied her. Couldn't help himself. "I can afford it, you know," he finally said, unable to resist the comment or the smile currently sliding across his lips.

Her gaze shot to his above the rim of her wineglass. "Afford what?"

"Whatever you wish to order. I'm curious. Do you even like crawfish?" Most people considered them an acquired taste, and frankly, she didn't look like the type.

The faintest hint of humor twinkled in her pale green gaze. She shrugged, forewent the "duh" act. "No," she admitted without the smallest trace of sheepishness. "Not really."

Tate chuckled, shifted in his chair. "You really are a piece of work, you know that?"

"I try."

"Now you'll be hungry. What was the point of that?"

"Oh, I won't be hungry." Her mouth tucked

into a secret smile and her brows rose significantly. "I happen to like chicken and sausage jambalaya."

A bark of laughter erupted from his throat.
Phantom balls, he thought again, once more reluctantly impressed with the devious workings of
her crafty mind. "Oh, that's rich. You ordered the
most expensive meal on the menu—one that you
don't even like, of all the pigheaded things—and
in addition to making me pay for it, you also expect me to share." He chuckled grimly. "That's
logical."

"No, I don't expect you to share," she corrected
amiably, lifting her glass to her lips. "I thought
we'd trade."

Tate's eyes widened. "Trade?"

She nodded serenely. "You know us women.
We're so—" her smooth brow puckered with exaggerated concentration "—fickle, I believe you
said. Yeah, that was definitely it. 'Fickle to the
point of being unable to make the most mundane
decisions.'"

He slouched back in his chair, scowled. "You're
not fickle—you're evil. Calculating. Vindictive,
sneaky and shrewd."

She laughed delightedly, as though he'd com-
plimented her. "Stop it," she chided. "You'll make
me blush."

Beyond making her angry, he hadn't quite figured out how to make her blush, but he knew it damn sure wouldn't happen with flattery. She was too damned cocky, too sure of her own intelligence, her own appeal. She was remarkably...like him, Tate realized with a shock of insight. Was that why he liked her so much? Because they shared many of the same traits? Hell, who knew? But the fact remained that she definitely appealed to him.

On some bizarre level, they'd clicked. She'd felt it, too, otherwise she wouldn't be trying so hard to avoid him, provoke, annoy and irritate him. Tate recognized those tactics and briefly wondered why thus far he'd only concentrated on the latter three with her. He definitely didn't want to avoid her.

In fact, he thought as his gaze traced the lush curve of her mouth, the feminine slope of her cheek, the closer he could get to her the better. A snake of heat writhed in his belly and slithered into his loins. A curious shiver slipped up his spine.

"What? No comeback?" she asked when he didn't readily reply. "Have I shocked you into silence?"

Tate absently fingered the stem of his wineglass, shook his head and laughed softly. "If learning that you piss like a guy didn't shock me into silence, then I can't imagine that anything else you'd have to tell me would." He feigned a startled look. "Wait. You're not a transvestite, are you? In the middle of a sex change?" He knew better, of course. Hell, he knew the difference between a man and a woman, knew beyond a shadow of a doubt that this one was the genuine article. His dick-dar wouldn't mislead him that way, he was sure of it.

"No," she drawled. "I can assure you I'm all girl."

Yeah. He'd noticed. Everything about her was ultrafeminine. But since they were on the subject… "I realize this is probably a little personal, but… How?" he asked skeptically. "How is it possible? You don't have a penis."

She grinned. "I'm aware of that, thanks. As for the how…" She shrugged. "It's a technique. I assure you, it can be done. It takes practice, but considering that we camped all summer—*every summer*—of my childhood and into my early teens, I taught myself. It was a necessity." She lifted a shoulder. "Besides, if my brothers could do it, then so could I."

Tate grinned, inordinately pleased with the insight. "So competing with men has been a lifelong trait then?"

She considered him for a moment and, though it could only be his imagination, she seemed to relax marginally. "I guess you could say that, yes."

He inclined his head. "I suspected as much."

"Yeah," she said drolly. "I'm sure you did."

"I did," Tate insisted. "I don't think you've realized it yet, but I am an authority on women. Ask anyone," he told her, gesturing magnanimously. "Ask the *New York Times*."

An ironic chuckle bubbled up her throat. "The only thing you're an authority on is bullshit."

Ah, he'd made her curse again. Another coup. "Maybe so," he conceded with a sigh. "But bullshit's lucrative."

"Too true, but that's not why you're into it." Her voice rang with matter-of-fact insight, as though the matter had been pondered, weighed and sorted and she was privy to his secrets, even some unknown to him. It unnerved the hell out of him.

He conjured a careless laugh, but it rang false even to his own ears. "Oh? What other reason could I possibly have?"

She gave him a probing look. Those calm green eyes seemed to be zeroing in on his most private thoughts, boring through barriers he'd carefully put into place. "I'm not sure yet," she said slowly. "But I know it's not the money. You have money. By all accounts Hatcher Advertising is doing quite well."

Tate looked up. So she *had* researched him to some degree. Actually, it was common knowledge that he owned an advertising firm. It would have been beyond ignorant not to capitalize on his recent success, not to take advantage of his fifteen minutes of fame. While he hadn't necessarily pitched his business, he'd managed to smoothly work it into several important interviews.

Since then his company had been flooded with accounts that primarily dealt with men's advertising. Deodorant, tools, hair care, trucks and SUVs, etc… You name it. If guys bought it, Tate had been given the job of advertising it. Ross Hartford, one of his good friends, was especially good at it as well and had been a tremendous asset in recent months. Ross, Tate thought reflectively, now there was another man's man. He could write his own book on the subject of women as well.

As for himself, Tate had no plans—beyond this next book, which he had already contracted—to write any more. Honestly, though he'd enjoyed the writing process, he didn't have the same passion for it as he did his primary business. He was a salesman. Liked to use his creative abilities in other capacities. He wanted his life back. He'd managed to squeeze in a call to Blake this afternoon and share that little tidbit again, but naturally his agent was more concerned with making sure he fulfilled his contractual obligations up to this point. He'd insisted that Tate keep him up to date, and planned to work up some ideas from his end as well, based on what Tate passed along.

"I do all right," Tate finally told her, tuning back in to the conversation.

"Which is why money wasn't the motivator. Something else drives you and your unflattering opinions of my sex." She quirked a brow. "Something personal. Care to share?" she asked lightly, as though it would be that easy.

He laughed, shrugged. "I'm an open book."

"To some degree. However—"

"Unlike you," Tate interrupted smoothly, eager for a subject change. "*You* are shrouded in mystery. Have many secrets. What brought about Chicks-In-Charge, for instance? And don't give me that line of bull about seeing the need," he told her. "It's more personal than that," he insisted meaningfully, throwing her words back at her. "And what's the deal with this Dex?" He frowned. "Why in God's name did you want a boyfriend who was into abstinence? One who didn't want to have sex?" he asked incredulously. Honestly, it was mind-boggling. A travesty. "Just a guess here, but I imagine that's pretty damned personal as well."

She paused and her lips slid into a familiar smirk. "Been dwelling on it, have you?"

"Dwelling? No. Considering. Yes." The waitress arrived with their food and instead of arguing with her about their meals, he immediately switched their plates. They were finally getting into some interesting issues and he didn't want any reason for her to change the subject. He took up his knife and fork and carved into the steak. "I mean, come on," he scoffed. "I've known women who like to take things slow—"

She snorted. "Bet you kicked them to the curb pretty darned quick, didn't you?"

"But to purposely pick a guy who isn't into it at all?" He grunted. "That's a *major* shift. That's got bad experience written all over it."

"Well, there you go," she said, spooning up a hearty bite of *his* jambalaya. "Mystery solved. That'll free up that brain cell and you can put it to work learning something about the opposite sex at my conference. Here's a title for your next book—*What Women Really—Truly—Want. Psst. I Got it Wrong Last Time.*"

Tate chuckled at the jibe. "So what happened?" he asked, unwilling to be deterred. "This is not book fodder," he felt compelled to add. He honestly wanted to know. "I'm just curious. Hell, can you blame me, after that scene in my room?"

She paused to consider him, and he felt the weight of that calm, steady stare. She finally sighed. "I suppose not." She took a sip of wine, seemed to weigh her words carefully. "You were right. Among other things, I'd just come out of a bad relationship. It seemed like a good decision at the time. Clearly, I was wrong."

Tate wanted to press her on the "among other things" point—he instinctively knew a significant revelation lurked in that innocuous phrase—but knew better. Instead, he focused on what she seemed to be willing to share. "So, from what I gathered, you initiated a seduction and he... wasn't interested." There was simply no delicate way to put it and the fact that he was even looking for one was out of character for him. Tate was a straight shooter. No hassles, no bullshit, no sugarcoating. It was part of his charm, what had made him so successful.

He watched her bite the inside of her cheek. "In a nutshell, yes."

Tate leaned back and exhaled a derisive snort. "Well, he was an idiot. If it makes you feel any better, I'd happily sleep with you."

Her eyes widened and she laughed out loud, a startled melodious chuckle that made a weird fluttering sensation take flight in his chest. "You'd sleep with anything that moved, but thanks anyway." Her eyes twinkled. "In your own boorish, insensitive way, I'm thinking that was a compliment."

"And in your own typical sarcastic way, you just repaid it with an insult," he drawled with mock chagrin. "I don't sleep with anything that moves, dammit. I happen to have very discerning tastes when it comes to choosing a lover." And he did. Hell, he didn't just dip his pen in any old inkwell. He had more respect for himself than that. Wasn't a slave to his baser needs, and frankly, didn't respect men who were.

Once again she paused to stare at him. A soft smile played over her lips and a wash of pink color painted her cheeks, from the alcohol, he decided. Whatever the reason, she looked particularly beautiful. His gaze dropped to her mouth, to that ripe bottom lip, specifically, and heat instantly flooded his groin. Oh, yeah. He'd definitely sleep with her. Fully intended to.

The last two guys she'd dated had obviously done a helluva number on her. One had shaken her up emotionally, the other had shaken her confidence. If anybody needed a long night of mindless, back-clawing, sweaty, frantic sex, it was her. Tate could try to tell himself that he'd be doing her a favor, giving her something that she'd even admitted that she needed, but it would be a self-serving lie.

He wanted her.

Some internal driving force beyond attraction told him that he had to have her. The need was there of course—fierce, intense, barely manageable—but it was more than that. He couldn't explain it any more than he could control it. He simply knew he had to have her. It was that he-man thing again. The bizarre phenomenon had struck him again when he'd taken her hand to help her out of the car. Touching her—even the most innocent contact—did something to him. That whole defend-protect-dominate thing roared through him, left him short of breath and a tingle in its wake.

"We should probably be heading back," she told him. Her voice was cool and calm as always, but he detected just the smallest hint of wariness in her gaze. She was good at reading him, Tate thought—too good, actually—and had evidently sensed the change in the air between them.

"Sure," he told her, tossing his napkin onto his plate. He smiled. "We've still got a few hands of poker to play, after all."

And after he beat her, they'd be playing a different sort of game, one that would be mutually—explosively—gratifying.

5

"So what are we playing?" Tate asked her.

Zora settled comfortably into her chair and schooled her expression into her poker face. Considering she usually wore one, it wasn't hard. "Five-card draw," she said with a negligent shrug, "unless you prefer some other variation."

Tate nodded. "Five-card works for me. Are you dealing, or am I?"

"You deal," Zora instructed. "It's your deck, after all." She'd inspected it of course, and to be honest, the idea that he traveled with his cards made her a smidge nervous—*everything* about him made her a smidge nervous—but she'd rather be roasted on a spit than admit it.

Tate competently shuffled. His long, blunt-tipped fingers effortlessly manipulated the cards, and she could easily imagine those same fingers working a similar magic on her. The floor lamp caught the golden highlights in his perpetually tousled hair, cast one side of his face in stark relief and the perfection of that silhouette was particularly mesmerizing. Made her fingers itch to trace the masculine slope of his cheek, the firm angle of his jaw, the rather full, sexy mouth. He looked unguarded, boyish and approachable.

In all honesty it was a miracle she'd been able to eat a morsel of food at all—even his, though that was definitely one of her brighter moments— given that her belly had been hot, quivery and muddled ever since she'd found him in the shower the night before and he'd caught her with those gorgeous eyes. Even realizing it was him, of all people, hadn't been as much of a deterrent to her wayward libido as it should have been.

He'd dogged her every step, had zinged her with that lazy, promising grin and, instead of sitting stoically across the table from him and resisting that considerable charm, she'd found herself responding, mellowing, softening, even. He might be a beast, she thought as something horrifyingly close to affection wormed its way into her thawing heart...but he was an adorable beast.

Zora inwardly groaned with frustration. Of all the guys in the world for her to want so desperately, why the hell had her usually sound mind failed her now, and latched on to him? *Him,* of all people? A guy who thought so little of her gender? A guy who'd capitalized on those opinions to the tune of thousands of dollars, who made a mockery of all she stood for, who annoyed the hell out of her? It was the height of irony.

Worse, the height of stupidity.

But Zora knew her limitations and knew enough about her own mind to realize that her intellect wasn't going to be any match for this keen—almost overpowering—sense of animal magnetism. Not this time, at any rate. Knew it, felt it. She let go a shuddering breath. Perversely, looked forward to it.

Her gaze slid to where his notebook sat on his bedside table. Would that she could just get a little peek at his notes, to see just what sort of spin he planned to put on this new book. To make sure that he kept his promise and kept her personal information out of it. To see if any of the things he'd heard today had seeped into that thick skull of his. She doubted it, of course, but if even one little morsel of wisdom had worked its way into his stubborn, arrogant head, then at least she'd feel marginally justified for this demonic attraction. It would mean that her radar wasn't completely faulty, that he *could* learn. That she *could* fix him.

Regardless, she knew he'd taken several notes. He'd made a point of letting her know, the insufferable wretch. He'd made a grand, deliberate show of taking notes during all of her workshops, and had even gone so far as to listen in on conversations he wasn't participating in, simply to hang on to her every word.

It was unnerving.

What had been even more unnerving was how easily he'd conned her into confiding in him, how easily it had come to her for that matter. She'd *wanted* to tell him, to explain, but she couldn't do it without ranting—exploding—because she'd kept those feelings beaten into submission for so long she knew that if she ever let them bubble up, she'd erupt like a dormant volcano.

Erupting to him was out of the question. It would be too damned humiliating. Too much of a loss of control. She'd fought too hard for it her entire life to give it up now.

Still, why couldn't she scream into her pillow, or vent her frustration in other ways? Why did letting go—admitting her emotions—feel like such a loss of control for her? She knew it would be cathartic, knew that channeling her irritation and anger into revenge wasn't healthy, even if it did manage to make her feel better. As much as she was loathe to admit it, she could pinpoint the exact time when she changed—that moment of helplessness behind that dugout. She'd never gotten past it. Had never really wanted to—after all, what doesn't kill you makes you stronger, right?—until recently.

Chicks-In-Charge had given her the venue, the confidence, independence and purpose. Her gaze slid to Tate. There was something about him that nudged her past control, something about *him*, in particular. What? Who knew? Irritation probably, Zora thought with a mental harrumph. God knows she'd never met a guy who annoyed her more.

Speaking of which… During dinner and their subsequent ride back to the hotel—with only a brief pit stop for beer, a prerequisite for playing poker, according to Tate—he'd managed to worm some pretty personal details out of her without admitting even the smallest hint about his own self. Not fair, Zora decided. That needed to be rectified and now seemed like just as good a time as any.

"We haven't talked stakes yet," she mentioned nonchalantly as he dealt the cards.

He looked up and smiled. Those unique amber eyes glowed with humor and some secret knowledge he possessed but wasn't quite ready to share. "I had something in mind, if you're game," he added, with just enough arrogance to make her thighs rigid.

"So do I, but let's hear yours first."

Tate pulled a long draw from his beer, then set the bottle aside. He slouched back into his chair, regarded her thoughtfully. She felt his gaze linger on her mouth, then drift down her neck and settle on her breasts just long enough to make her nipples tingle and pearl behind the slick fabric of her bra. A sluggish heat wound through her limbs and a steady beat commenced between her legs. In that instant she knew what he was going to suggest—what he'd ask for—and, to her unending disquiet, she couldn't decide if she was offended or thrilled.

His somewhat darkened gaze tangled with hers once more. "For every hand I win, I get one kiss and one intimate touch."

Zora conjured a smirk, but knew it fell short of the mark. "And if I win?"

The corner of his mouth tucked into a sexy smile. "I'll play fair. You can have a kiss and an intimate touch, too."

She chuckled, she couldn't help it. "Well, that's not what I had in mind."

He winced. "Damn. It figures." He sighed. "Okay. If hell freezes over, pigs fly and Lady Luck dances on both of your shoulders, then just what exactly is it that you want? And, for the record, making me leave *isn't* an option."

She hadn't even thought of that, which just went to show how much he'd rattled her. That should have been her first thought—getting him out of here. Not trying to unearth his shrunken, neglected conscience. Harassing him, converting him—presently, doing both heartily appealed to her—or anything else for that matter. Him being here was a threat, and yet the idea of him leaving didn't seem to sit well either.

Zora resisted the urge to groan. He'd totally confused her. "I want some information. For every hand I win, I get to ask a question and you have to answer honestly, truthfully, without any of your customary bullshit."

Tate studied her and the smile he'd been wearing thinned a fraction. "What sort of questions? Personal questions?"

She nodded. "What other kind would I be interested in? I want to know the stuff I can't find on the Internet." She waited while he considered, then finally grinned with victory. "Not so confident when you have something important to lose, are you, Boy Genius?" She laughed.

He looked up and she knew she'd hit a nerve. The playful humor had been replaced with a hard, competitive smile. "I'm not the least bit worried."

Zora chewed her lip skeptically. "I can see that. That's why you're hesitating. What? Afraid you'll lose?"

The change that came over him was swift and unexpected. He still wore a smile, but it was tight with tension and every trace of humor had vanished from his gaze. What? Zora wondered. What had she said? She'd simply needled him, the same way he'd needled her. She'd accused him of hesitating, of being afraid, of possibly losing. One of those things—if not all—had set him off. It was an exaggerated reaction, to be sure, and it made her doubly determined to find out what made him tick.

He looked up and caught her staring, and she watched him struggle to pull his typically amiable mask back into place. It was one of the most heart-wrenching things she'd ever witnessed. Tate Hatcher had been hurt—deeply—and had big secrets. She knew it, and now, despite her better judgment, was determined to know what they were. How else was she supposed to fix him, if she didn't know the problem?

He struggled with a laugh. "I don't know what you're thinking, but I know that I'm not going to like it."

Zora grinned, refused to reveal any of her thoughts. She consulted her hand, then slid two cards across the table. "If we're agreed on the stakes, then I need two."

"We're agreed." Seemingly relaxing once more, Tate obliged, then adjusted his own hand. "Well?" he asked. "Ready to lay down?"

"You first."

Tate smiled, then spread his cards. "Two pair, fives and nines."

Zora didn't betray so much as a flicker of victory, merely showed her hand. "Three of a kind. There's ice water in hell," she remarked drolly.

He chuckled. "Okay. So you won one," he conceded. "Ask your question."

Zora didn't even have to think about it. She'd been wondering for months. Ever since his confounded book came out, the same question had been burning a hole in the back of her head. She exhaled mightily, asked it in one long whoosh. *"What woman did a number on you?"* It was the closest thing to a wail she'd uttered since she was a child.

He cackled, actually threw back his head and laughed delightedly. "Ah, hell. I thought you were gonna ask me an *original* question. I've been asked that more than a dozen times. Women automatically assume there's a reason for what I think—for the last time, there's not." He said it with the exaggerated patience of a parent trying to impart an important bit of wisdom to a toddler. "I've never had my heart broken, haven't been the victim of unrequited love, none of that crap. I just took a few little unflattering ideas, exaggerated them until I knew they'd appeal to men and sold the damned book." He leaned forward. "There's no big secret, no grand horrific thing in my past." He shifted and she watched the slightest flicker of unreadable emotion flash so quickly in those whiskey eyes that for a moment she thought she might have imagined it.

But she knew she hadn't. Fine, Zora thought. He thought she'd wasted a question, but that telling little glimpse into his soul—she'd decided he *did* possess one—had given her the information she'd needed to ask the *right* question the next time.

She twisted her lips into what she knew he'd wrongfully assume was irritation. "Just deal, would you?"

Tate quickly shuffled and doled out the cards once more. He took another draw of his beer, then grinned, that confident mask in place once more. "How many?"

Zora consulted her cards. They sucked. She wasn't going to get to ask another question with this sort of hand. Which meant he'd win and he'd kiss her. An involuntary shiver crawled over her scalp. "Three."

Tate passed her cards, then adjusted his own hand. He only took one, which rattled her nerves. "What have you got?"

"A pair of jacks."

Tate laid down his hand, showing a pair of nines. She'd won again.

Zora smiled. She turned and cast a dramatic look out the window. "Wow," she breathed. "Did you see that? A pig just flew by." She tsk-tsked under her breath, shook her head. "You're really not as good at this as you led me to believe."

"My time will come."

"Yeah, well, you'd better hope it comes in this next hand, because after that, we're finished."

His eyes widened. "What?"

"You said a few. A few is three," Zora explained patiently.

"Or more."

"Wrong." She glanced at her watch. "It's getting late and I have an early schedule."

He pondered that for a moment. "Fine. Then we play again tomorrow night."

"That's awfully brave," she teased. "By the time we're finished, I'll know all of your secrets as well as your PIN codes and credit-card numbers."

"Or I'll have you in bed," he countered in that typical, unrepentant, matter-of-fact way that never ceased to amaze her.

A flash of heat hit the tops of her thighs and a startled laugh bubbled up her throat. Her gaze flew to his. She knew that's where this was heading, why he'd bet a kiss and intimate touch, but having him glibly announce his agenda was a bit disconcerting. Refreshing, too, if she were honest. Still, she felt like she should be outraged by his audacity, should form some sort of protest.

But that wasn't in keeping with her character, so instead she merely summoned an indulgent smile. "Confident, aren't you?"

He nodded, smiled that lazy smile that had the singular ability to melt her brain. "You want me."

"Not any more than you want me," she returned. "And you don't like it either."

He hesitated, seemed to search for the right words. "It's inconvenient. Stupid, even." His gaze dropped to her mouth, lingered long enough to make her lick her lips. "But I can't help it and I'm not accustomed to denying myself. Any more than you are, if I'm right."

Honestly, this was the most surreal conversation. She couldn't believe they were sitting here, relatively calmly discussing this attraction, *discussing* becoming lovers. Her palms itched and the image of sitting astride his naked body, riding him until her body shuddered with climax, materialized behind her lids.

She did want him. Desperately. More than she'd ever wanted anything in her life. But there were things she needed to know first, had to, in order to surrender to the attraction.

Zora tucked her hair behind her ear. "I believe that it's my turn to ask a question."

Tate just grinned, gestured wearily. "So you're not ready to end the dance?" He shot a glance over to the bed. "We could be in there right now and I could make you come within ninety seconds of getting you there. You want it, I know you do." He sighed. "But I'll go another round with you. Ask away."

I could make you come within ninety seconds of getting you there.... Zora knew she should move right along to her question, knew that by hesitating she might as well wave a red flag in front of a bull—Tate wouldn't miss it, he was too damned quick—but the idea that, at any given time, she could be ninety seconds away from an orgasm with this man had taken root in her poor, sexually deprived mind and she could scarcely think of anything else. Had another guy said that to her, she would have been convinced it was all brag— hot air—without the skill to back it up.

But with Tate she knew better.

She instinctively knew he could do it. Her breath left her in a shallow sigh and a slow, sluggish heat slipped languidly through her veins. Powerful words, those, particularly to a woman who hadn't had a hot body between her legs in more than a year.

"Zora?"

She looked up, caught his shrewd grin.

"What about that question?"

Question… Question… Oh, yeah. She cleared her throat, attempted to clear her foggy brain. "Out of all the women you have ever known—period—" she emphasized, "every woman, which one—if any—do you have the most contempt for?"

A bit of the cockiness faded from his gaze and a shutter dropped into place, preventing her from reading him.

"What's with all these 'women' questions?" Tate countered, clearly exasperated.

She smiled sweetly. "When you win a hand, you can ask me."

He snorted. "When I win one I'm going to kiss you until the last thing you want to use your tongue for is *idle talk*," he said meaningfully. "Talking's overrated, especially when a woman has the kind of mouth you do." He leaned forward, lowered his voice and she felt herself being sucked in, intoxicated. "Haven't you ever noticed that I stare at your mouth all the time? It's sexy. Makes me so damned hot I'm practically coming out of my pants." He cocked his head toward the bed again. "Come on, let's forget this," he urged softly. He reached across the table and ran the pad of his thumb over her bottom lip. Zora gasped, momentarily let her lids drift shut. "Ninety seconds," he said again. "Come on," he whispered. An invitation, an entreaty...the promise of sin.

From the dimmest recesses of her mind she knew he was trying to sidetrack her. Did he want her? Yes, he did. She knew he did. Still, the fact that he'd go to the trouble to up the seduction mode now, when he'd been content to drag it out a few minutes ago, told her what she needed to know. He didn't want to answer her question, but thought enough of his word once he'd given it to be truthful.

Her tongue felt curiously thick—about as thick as the sensual haze presently encircling her brain—but Zora finally managed to pull it together. "What woman do you have the most contempt for?" she repeated doggedly. The answer lay here—she knew it.

He leaned back and rolled his eyes. Sighed tiredly. "You're going to read too much into it. You're going to try and analyze me and I'll *hate* it." He muttered a hot oath.

"I'll keep my thoughts to myself," she conceded.

Tate expelled a bitter breath, looked away, then finally gave her his full attention once more. "Fine. The one woman that I hold the most contempt for isn't an old girlfriend or lover—it's my mother." He took up his beer and pulled a long swallow. He gazed out the window. "Now analyze away."

Silence thundered between them and Zora couldn't have been any more shocked than if he'd slapped her. His mother? Naturally, the question that burned on her tongue was why, but she knew better than to ask. Knew better than to speak, and definitely knew better than to betray a single inkling of the pity that automatically squeezed her heart.

He quirked a brow, studied her for a moment. "Aren't you going to ask why?"

She swallowed. "I haven't won another hand yet."

"I'll save you the trouble so that we can move on. I'll give you the abbreviated facts, and then I never want to talk about this again. Understood?"

Zora nodded.

"She left for milk—for *my* cereal—when I was nine and never came back. My dad never got over it and never came out of the bottle. He died two years later—alcohol poisoning—and I moved in with my grandparents. Have I heard from her? No. Do I want to hear from her? Hell no. Is she the reason I act the way I do, say the things I say? No. But that's what you're going to think, and you can have at it. You just don't want me to be an asshole because you're attracted to me." A hard smile caught his lips. "News flash—I'm not an asshole, but I'm *not* going to let any woman lead me around by the nose—or the balls—or any other appendage. *The end.*" He gave the cards another shuffle. "Now let's play."

For the first time in her life Zora didn't find any victory in being right. She'd known that something had happened to make him think so little of the opposite sex, but she'd just naturally assumed that it was the product of a soured relationship. That his mother had deserted him had never occurred to her. It didn't take much to fill in what few blanks he'd left, nor did it take a Ph.D. in psychology to understand the ramifications. His mother had left—which had made him feel unlovable—and his father had evidently not been strong enough to cope with her desertion and take the lead role in raising an impressionable young boy.

Though she knew he'd be offended by any sort of emotion from her—other than desire—Zora had to repeatedly, forcibly check the impulse to try and ease his pain. Despite the bravado, she knew it was there. Knew that his commitment issues were a direct result of a combination of his father's weakness and his mother's desertion. After all, if his mother couldn't love him, then who could, right? Furthermore, seeing a father wrecked by love couldn't have created a healthy impression, either.

Was he going to admit it? Hell no, because admitting it equaled failure and weakness, neither of which were tolerable to him. Zora resisted the urge to roll her eyes. She certainly understood that. She'd been guilty of that offense as well.

She steadied her trembling fingers and withdrew three cards from her hand, slipped them across the table. "Three," she said needlessly, simply because the silence was closing in on them.

Tate saw to her request, then tended to his own hand. "Well?" he asked.

"Three of a kind," she said, fanning the cards on the table for his perusal.

Tate's gaze dropped to her mouth and he licked his lips. She knew then that she'd lost. That he'd managed to trump her hand. Without a word, he put his cards down—faceup so that she could see his full house—then very calmly, very deliberately, pushed his chair back and stood.

He was about to claim his kiss, Zora thought as her belly churned with excited tingles and her breath left her in a small whoosh of anticipation. He was about to claim his kiss…and, she thought dimly, undoubtedly her heart.

6

AT LAST, TATE THOUGHT. *He could finally put that ripe mouth to better use.* He calmly laid down his winning hand, then just as calmly stood. Then, without any hesitation whatsoever at all, he walked around the table, grabbed the arms of her chair and swiftly turned it away from the table to face him.

He dropped to his knees, spread her thighs in order to put himself closer to her and smoothly framed her face with his hands.

Then he leaned forward and fitted his mouth to hers.

The sweet taste of her exploded on his tongue. Gooseflesh raced from his feet to his crown and that wild, all-consuming he-man sensation took hold once more. *Defend, dominate, nurture and protect.* If merely touching her before had affected him, then kissing her was practically turning him inside out.

His entire body tingled, every cell sang with some sort of primal recognition. The emotion was as thrilling as it was terrifying and since admitting fear of any sort was out of the question, Tate told himself that he was punishing her for making him think about his mother, for making him talk about her, as though she could claim credit for any sentiment he possessed aside from contempt and indifference.

His fingers trembled out of irritation.

His insides quaked because she'd annoyed him.

He'd felt this way before—this sensation was nothing new—and just because he couldn't recall it didn't mean that she was special, that just because he craved her like a junkie craved a fix didn't mean that she'd wormed her way into his affections. She couldn't have—he didn't possess any.

She annoyed him, irritated him, made him crazy. A guy would have to be insane to entertain any thought beyond taking her to bed. Tate knew these things—knew them—and yet all the warnings he heaped upon his helpless mind were meaningless in the face of being with her. Tasting her, kissing her, feeling her hair slide over the backs of his hands, the bittersweet flutter of her lashes against his cheek.

Without warning, Zora suddenly sighed into his mouth and he savored her surrender, ate that breath of supplication like a death-row inmate savoring a last meal, smiled against her plum-soft lips.

He had her.

She leaned forward and eagerly tunneled her fingers into his hair, kneaded his scalp, played at his nape and the sensitive area behind his ears. Another sigh hissed into their joined mouths, this one a part groan of satisfaction, of desperate hunger. Her hands left his hair, then found his face. She fitted her palms to his cheeks, almost reverently, and angled his head so that she could better align their mouths, fed at him until his loins throbbed and the only thing that prevented his dick from swelling right up out of the top of his shorts was his belt.

Tate moved closer, couldn't get enough of her. Her body was small, curvy, soft, yet strong. He loved the feel of her, the taste of her. There was nothing hesitant about the way she moved her greedy hands over his body, nothing shy about the bold push of her tongue into his mouth.

"You've got thirty seconds," she murmured thickly.

"What?" Tate asked, licking a path down the side of her neck.

"Now just twenty-five. You'd better get on with it. I'd recommend that 'intimate touch.'"

It took a precious second for his muddled brain to comprehend, but only half of one to move into action. He slid two buttons from their closures, brushed her shirt aside and latched his greedy mouth onto the peak of her breast through the flimsy fabric of her bra.

She gasped, arched her back, automatically pushing the creamy globe farther into his mouth. Her scent, something musky and sweet—woman—invaded his nostrils, and if he'd ever smelled a more compelling aroma, he couldn't recall it.

Tate tugged at her waistband, felt her belly tremble as he worked the button loose, the zipper down. Hot skin, moist panties...ah, Tate thought as he smiled against her nipple, heaven. He parted her drenched folds, dragged his fingers over the wet, velvety skin, then knuckled her clit.

Her mouth opened in a startled gasp of pleasure and she squirmed against him, moved her body against his hand. "Fifteen," she managed to croak.

Tate grinned, upped the tempo, then delivered the coup de grâce. He slid two fingers deep inside her, hooked them around until he discovered her hot button, then with the crown of her breast pulled deeply into his mouth, he simultaneously sucked hard, knuckled hard and pressed hard.

Predictably, she shattered.

A long silent scream formed on her mouth, her body trembled violently and she spasmed tightly against his fingers. Tate held firm, gently worked her as she rode out the release, waited for the tremors to stop, until every last morsel of release had been milked from her responsive body.

She melted against the back of the chair, a gorgeous, sated smile on her equally gorgeous face. Her breath still came in jagged little puffs, her lips were swollen from his kisses, and the glow of recent orgasm painted her cheeks. Neck still arched, she chuckled helplessly and gazed at the ceiling. "That was— I can't believe—" She paused and looked at him. "Well done," she said meaningfully, her voice ringing with enough awe to make more than the head on his shoulders swell.

Tate's loins were locked in Satan's own hell and his dick was so damned hard he feared it might burst. Relieving him, ironically, didn't seem to have occurred to her. "Thanks," he managed.

He leaned forward once more, captured her mouth with his. He kissed her slow and deep, pulled her hips closer to the edge of the chair and rocked against her. Her breath caught again and another wanton chuckle—had he ever heard anything so damned sexy? Tate wondered dimly— bubbled up her throat.

She wormed her way closer, worked his shirt free of his pants and slid her cool hands up over his skin. He shivered, quaked, burned. Those small capable hands mapped his back, trekked slowly around and smoothed over his chest, his belly. She scored his nipples with her fingernails, tore her mouth away from his and bent and licked a hot trail down the side of his neck, nipped at his shoulder.

Tate's hands were equally greedy for the feel of her skin. He finished with the buttons on her shirt, pushed the garment off and went to work on the bra. He'd just undone the clasp when he felt the brush of her fingers at the waistband of his pants. A startled breath hissed past his suddenly clenched teeth.

"I don't know if I can get you off in ninety seconds," she murmured as his zipper whined in the silence. "But I'm going to give it a try." An evil little smile curled her mouth. "You know how competitive I am." And with that loaded comment, her hot hand closed around his equally hot dick and twenty seconds later—he knew, because for some unknown ignorant reason, he counted—he came harder than he ever had in his life. The climax rocketed through him, blasted from his loins like a bullet down the barrel of a gun.

Tate sat back on his haunches—there was no

way in hell he could stand—and waited for his breathing to return to normal.

"Ah," Zora sighed. "A new record. That'll be your time to beat next time."

"Come to bed and I'll get right to work on it," he murmured suggestively.

Zora looked over his shoulder and, curious, Tate turned and followed her gaze. The bedside clock. She swiftly went to work setting her clothing to rights. "I would, however, I was afraid this very thing would happen and I sort of arranged—"

The rest of what she said was lost as a knock sounded at what could only be her door.

She winced. "That's Frankie."

Tate wanted to wail. They'd barely gotten started! The best was yet to come! "It's a little late for a watchdog, isn't it?" he asked drolly.

She tucked her shirt in, shot him a look. "I didn't think— I…" She shrugged helplessly. "It's done. I'm sorry."

Tate moved forward and pulled her into the circle of his arms, lowered his voice. He nuzzled her ear. "Come back when she leaves."

"She's not leaving. She's pulling duty all night."

That was as annoying as it was flattering. "Then tomorrow night? Poker again?"

"You sure you wanna lose again?"

Tate chuckled. "Baby, we both got off. How's that losing?"

Frankie knocked again, more insistent this time, and called her friend's name.

Zora leaned forward and kissed him. "Gotta go. G'night."

"Good night," Tate called softly.

FRANKIE TOOK ONE LOOK at her, then calmly walked to the connecting door and gave the lock a vicious, pointed twist. She plopped onto the end of the bed. "Have you lost your mind?" she wailed quietly. "Have you completely gone around the bend?"

Zora knew Frankie's concern was founded, however, as she'd just had the first guy-induced orgasm she'd had in more than a year, Frankie might as well be talking to the wall. She knew there'd be ramifications, knew that consorting with the enemy was probably one of the stupidest things she'd ever done…but for the first time in her life, she didn't care.

Zora pulled a nightgown out of one of the drawers, headed for the bathroom. "I'll be back out in a minute."

When she came back out, she found Frankie dressed and ready for bed as well, her expression just as disgusted and mulish as it had been when Zora'd left the room.

Frankie stared at her, waiting to resume the conversation. "Well?" she finally demanded.

Zora sank onto the end of the bed. "It's crazy, I know." She shrugged helplessly. "But I like him."

"Like him?" Frankie repeated, outraged. "What's there to like?" She leaned forward. "You know, when we were just dealing with the sexual attraction, I wasn't that worried. You're horny—have been horny for months on end—and, honestly, it was time for you to get back in the saddle. But this?" Her eyes widened and she jerked her finger toward the wall. "*Him?* Come on, Zora! This has got heartache written all over it—yours."

"I said I liked him," Zora explained calmly. "I didn't say anything about his-and-hers towels."

"Not to mention the other ramifications. If the women at this conference found out that you were sleeping with Tate Hatcher—"

"I'm not sleeping with Tate Hatcher—" *yet*, Zora mentally added "—and he's not likely to tell even if I were. His credibility would be ruined as well."

Frankie rolled her eyes. "For someone to be so smart, to have it all together, you can really miss a big point now and again."

Zora stilled. "What?" she asked cautiously.

"Zora, Tate's credibility isn't on the line. If he bags you and tells, he's a stud! He's the man! He put you in your place—right on your back! Don't you see?" she asked, her voice rising with every point. She snorted. "He has nothing to lose but a few hours sleep. You, on the other hand, are jeopardizing *everything*." She gestured helplessly. "Believe me, no one thinks you need to get laid more than I do, but letting Tate Hatcher do the laying is…risky. You better be sure of where you stand before you let this go any further."

Zora nodded thoughtfully. She knew everything Frankie had just said was the truth, knew that her friend had brought up several key points and knew that she should be worried, but curiously, she wasn't.

Had Tate planned to ruin her, he could have done that already. Furthermore—and she had no idea why she felt this way—but she simply knew that he had no hidden agenda. He'd been forthright and honest to the point of being tactless, had made no secret of why he was here or why he wanted her. He'd been nothing but honest with her. Was she being naive? Had that marvelous orgasm ruined her brain? Zora paused to consider, replayed their conversations. No, she didn't think so.

After a minute, she said as much to Frankie. "I know you think I've lost my mind, but I just don't think that's his angle. He's looking for research, true, but he's not using me personally. He gave me his word." And though she couldn't explain exactly why, she believed him. He was too damned honest to lie about it.

"For your sake, I hope not." That settled, a wicked smile curled her lips. "So what happened tonight? If you didn't get laid, then why did you walk in here with that shit-eatin' grin on your face?"

A pulse of heat hit her loins, remembering. "Just because I didn't get laid doesn't mean that I didn't get off."

Frankie whooped quietly and slapped her hand against the mattress. "Hallelujah, praise God and pass the molasses!"

Zora shared Tate's ninety-second promise. "It's not all talk, either, my friend," Zora said, reliving that particular moment when he did that clever little thing with his finger. "For me, it was less than thirty seconds."

"Yeah, well, you hadn't had one in a long time," Frankie pointed out. "The first time was bound to be easy. Tomorrow night will be the true test." She quirked a knowing brow. "I'm assuming you'll see him again tomorrow night."

Zora let go a small breath. She nodded. "Yeah. We're playing poker again," she said drolly. "Which is actually a good thing. There are still a few things I'd like to know."

Frankie gave her puzzled look. "What are you talking about?"

Zora gave her their rules and shared the tidbit she'd managed to worm out of him about his mother. "Hell, Frankie, no wonder he's so messed up." Who wouldn't be? she thought, her chest aching for the hurt little boy, the wounded man.

Frankie paused, seemingly mulling it over. "That's pretty damned bad. And for *his cereal?* As an adult he's worked out that was merely an excuse, but can you imagine the kind of guilt heaped upon a nine-year-old conscience." Frankie scowled, huffing a disgusted breath. "What a twisted, selfish bitch. He undoubtedly blamed himself for everything, her leaving, his father dying." She shot Zora a look. "That would definitely create some issues. If you decide to really pursue this, are you prepared to deal with them?"

Her goal had been to fix him, Zora thought as her heart swelled with compassion for the broken little boy he'd been. If she did decide to pursue this, she'd do whatever it took to deal with whatever lingering issues.

Zora finally nodded. "Yeah," she said thoughtfully. "I am."

"Then it's settled then. Trust your instincts. If you think he's on the up-and-up, then that's good enough for me. I'm not as sure as you are, but I don't have to be. It's your heart on the line." She paused. "Which brings me to my next question. Is this a he's-hot-forbidden-and-fascinating kind of like? Or is this a he-makes-my-heart-flutter-potential-mate kind of like?"

Zora stilled, mulled over the two options Frankie had given her and couldn't decide. She lifted her shoulders in a helpless shrug. "A little of both," she confided smally, somewhat afraid to admit it. "To be honest, I've…I've just never felt this way before. He evokes so many emotions, I have no idea. He makes me crazy," she growled. "But I like him." It was the most she was willing to admit at this point, couldn't bear to think about possibly falling in love with the obstinate beast.

Frankie gave her a long look and issued the same warning she'd given her yesterday. *"Be careful."*

7

"GOOD AFTERNOON," Zora called to the room at large. *"Welcome to How to Combat Men and Their Ignorant Opinions."* She smiled and held up his book. "I created this workshop after reading Mr. Hatcher's book because it's precisely this sort of mentality that we at Chicks-In-Charge are fighting." Her gaze drifted to Tate and a ghost of a smile shaped her lips. That faint curve of her mouth sent a bolt of heat sizzling through his blood. "This book, while funny and entertaining—*to men*—" she added pointedly "—is chock-full of ignorant, outdated, frankly *moronic* opinions." She paused and cast Tate a meaningful glance. "Pay attention, Mr. Hatcher. Here's where you might actually learn something...and you can thank me with a dedication," she added sweetly.

Oh, yeah, Tate thought. He'd thank her. Right after he throttled her. Honestly, it never occurred to him that she'd abandon her principles and come around to his way of thinking—frankly, he wouldn't respect her if she did—however, did she have to continue to roast him? Her hens and chicks had been pecking at him all day, admonishing him for every little presumed slight, telling him their stories. Some were quite horrific—sexual harassment, bypassed promotions, physical abuse. All with the same common denominator—a man.

In the grand scheme of things, he supposed he could see where his book would cause a heated debate among this group, could see where it would ruffle a few feathers.

But honestly, it wasn't like he was promoting those kinds of behaviors. Just inflaming them, a little-heeded voice whispered. Just belittling small gripes so that ultimately larger ones would be ignored or mocked. Tate shifted uncomfortably. Tried to put the unsettling idea out of his head. He wasn't hurting anyone, dammit, he insisted silently. It had been a joke, nothing harmful in that.

He felt his cell vibrate at his waist, smoothly snagged the phone and answered the call. He knew before he looked at the display who it'd be—Blake. Wondering again if he'd made any progress on a hook. Tate had been giving him reports a couple of times a day. What more could he want? Oh, yeah, he thought grimly. The book.

"Hello," he whispered softly with a covert look around the room.

"Can you talk?"

"Er…no, but I can listen. I'm in a workshop. One of Zora's." The lady next to him sent him a reproachful glance. Tate smiled and gestured helplessly.

"Good. Being in a workshop gathering stuff you can use is good. Speaking of which, have you gotten much you can use?"

"Some," Tate lied.

"Because—and I know you're tired of hearing this, Tate—but we're getting down to the wire here. You've got to have a proposal ready in a couple of weeks, and so far you don't seem to have gotten a firm grasp on this next story at all."

He was right, Tate thought. He *was* tired of hearing this. He massaged the bridge of his nose.

"Personally," Blake continued, "I think that you need to take the penis-envy approach—I keep thinking about Zora Anderson being able to pee like a guy and it's…unnerving. You've got something there. Work with it. Or better still, just work."

"I'm trying," Tate muttered tightly, then disconnected. Hell, he knew what he was supposed to be doing here, knew what was at stake. He didn't need Blake breathing down his neck every few hours.

Mildly annoyed, he tuned back in to the workshop, listened as Zora systematically tore apart his book, the vindictive she-devil. He felt his lips twitch.

But oh, what a gorgeous she-devil. With Blake's work edict still ringing in his ears, Tate felt a bit guilty just sitting here staring at her—he should be taking notes, pondering the next bedamned book—but he just couldn't help himself.

Today she wore a pale yellow linen suit and a pair of strappy sandals. That flame-colored hair had been pulled up into a neat knot on the back of her head and few fiery tendrils had worked loose and brushed the intriguing nape of her neck. She'd managed to seamlessly meld classy and sexy and the overall effect made him restless in his seat. Made something curiously reminiscent of pride expand in his chest.

Just like yesterday, he'd followed her around, had hung on to every word because—for reasons still unknown to him—she simply fascinated him. Listening to how that keen, diabolical mind worked was one of the most interesting things he'd ever encountered. Kissing that sweet, sultry mouth and feeling her climax around his fingers had been the single most erotic thing he'd ever experienced.

He couldn't wait for a repeat performance,

couldn't wait to feel those tight feminine muscles clamp around him as he pumped in and out of her. Every reaction she pulled out of him was exaggerated. With her, he felt everything more— to the nth degree—be it irritation or lust, and every variation in between.

Last night after she'd retreated to her room, Tate had lain in his lonely bed and tried to figure out just what about Zora Anderson did it for him. What made her so different? What compelled him to watch her every move? She was hot, and smart and guarded, all of which appealed to him. But there was something more, some indefinable something that he could feel and not name. It was *that* something that gave him pause, made him feel as though his body was growing out of his skin, his brain too big for his skull. He chuckled darkly. His dick too big for his pants.

That had certainly been the case last night. Despite the fact that he'd lost two hands of poker and had been forced to answer her confounded questions—which, on a fun scale, he'd rank right up there with a rectal exam, by the way—he'd barely been able to focus on anything outside of kissing her. He'd never in his life wanted to taste a woman more. It was odd how a mouth that was capable of delivering a steady stream of sarcastic acid could taste so damned sweet. Odd how slipping his tongue into that mouth made him alternately burn and quake. And even odder still how easily they'd talked about wanting each other.

That had definitely been a first. Tate was usually vocal about what he wanted. Playing games, beating around the bush—that's how breakdowns in communication occurred. If he thought it or wanted it, he simply said so. There were times when he'd been accused of being tactless, thoughtless, even, but in the end, the people he dealt with were usually thankful for his honesty.

Zora, he knew, kept her guard up, wore a continual poker face and guarded her thoughts and feelings with what he could only imagine had to be a daunting vigilance. That she'd felt comfortable enough with him to admit to their attraction told him many things, the most important of which was how desperately she wanted him as well. Tate knew beyond a shadow of a doubt that, like him, if she could control the attraction, she would. A slow smile rolled around his lips. Given that, one could assume he was irresistible. At least to her, at any rate.

"What's so funny, Mr. Hatcher?"

Startled, Tate looked up. Zora wore a faint smirk, had crossed her arms over her chest. He shifted, tried to look as though he'd been paying attention. A futile effort since every disapproving eye in the room was now focused on him. "I'm sorry?"

For the first time that poker face slipped and he could tell that she was having a royal ball at his expense. Roasting him wasn't enough—she fully intended to burn his ass to a crisp.

"What part of my last comment did you find amusing, I wonder? Would you like to tell us?"

Tate grinned, rubbed the back of his neck. "Actually, I would if I could, but the truth is I wasn't paying attention. I was thinking about something else." He purposely let his gaze drop to her mouth and sent her a significant look, lowered his voice. "Would you like me to share?"

Though he knew she took his meaning, not a flicker of emotion betrayed her face. "I think not."

"Oh, I wouldn't mind," he readily assured, purposely turning her game to his advantage, trying to make her crack again.

"I'm sure you wouldn't," she returned smoothly. "However, I have a workshop to conclude." She turned her attention back to the group as a whole. "The single most important bit of advice that I can give you—that you should take away from this conference and Chicks-In-Charge as a whole is this—*independence*. I have a friend right now who is in a terrible work situation, but she's actively positioning herself where she can, if not be her own boss, then at least get away from the one she currently has. You've all met Frankie," she reminded them. "Frankie's last promotion went to the bagel girl—and she worked for her *father*." Zora's lips curled with bitter humor. "Independence, ladies. Take control of your finances, your health, your relationships, your *lives*. You can do it alone, but by working together, we can do it better." Her gaze drifted to Tate once more and she smiled. "I don't know about the rest of you," she said loftily, "but I'll get my own door."

There it was again, Tate thought. His shrieking conscience. All this time he'd been bemoaning the fact that women had taken exception to the door comment, but—and, oh, would she love this— Tate had just realized that it really wasn't about the door at all. The door merely symbolized a bigger issue—disrespect.

Tate stood and prepared to leave. Reorganizing his opinions was disturbing business and he'd just as soon do it away from prying, too-perceptive eyes. Namely Zora's. He could feel that calm, cool stare boring into the side of his head, tunneling for his most secret thoughts. If she perceived even the slightest chink in his armor, she'd pounce. He knew it.

"Don't forget, ladies," she called sweetly. "Educate him. Stick to him like glue if need be."

Five seconds later he was surrounded by a brood of chicks. Hopelessly seething, Tate ambled slowly toward the door, purposely taking his time so that their paths would intersect. He smiled benignly, though inwardly he wanted to scream, wanted to punish her with passion again. Make her so hot she'd beg him for deliverance, so crazy that she'd admit to any wrong, perceived or true. "Does this mean that you're going to stick to me like glue tonight?" he asked silkily where only she could hear.

He watched a corner of her mouth hint at a smile, felt that faint grin land a punch of heat in his groin. She sighed softly. "Like liquid cement."

Tate blinked. Well, okay then, he thought as visions of her naked body glued to his materialized with speedy efficiency in the mini-theater of his mind. She was forgiven. In fact, he looked forward to forgiving her again and again.

Tonight.

"...OH, IT WAS THE FUNNIEST thing. We literally followed him into the bathroom," one of the Chick attendees confided gleefully. "Like we were gonna let a little thing like a pair of pants on a door stop us," she joked. "Honestly, I couldn't tell you if he's had a change of heart and learned anything, but we've sure managed to aggravate the heck out of him."

Zora grinned, imagined Tate being tailed into the men's room by a group of women all determined to reform him. "Aggravating works, too," Zora told her. "Just keep it up. We've only got a little more time to do what we can do. I truly appreciate all your efforts." Between wearing him down and actually giving him some meatier topics to ponder, hopefully he'd come around to her way of thinking. Or so she hoped.

Wearing a somewhat secret smile, Zora strolled away from the group. Without warning, Tate appeared from behind a huge potted palm, stuffed his hands into his pockets and fell in step beside her. "You are *really* enjoying this, aren't you? I mean, it's like Christmas has come early, you've won the lottery and have been guaranteed good parking karma for the rest of your life."

Zora laughed. "It's entertaining."

"Entertaining?" he echoed, his voice climbing. "Those eager beavers followed me into the bathroom. I had to unbutton my pants to make them leave."

Zora barely smothered a laugh, continued to stroll through the lobby to the bank of elevators. "I'm surprised. I would have thought that'd make them hang around."

He depressed the call button for the elevator.

"I thought I was alone, but guess what? I wasn't. One of your determined hens rapped on the door, and—" he chuckled darkly "—lemme tell you, I don't envy who's on bathroom duty tonight. You might be able to write your name in the snow, princess, but I bet you can't write *shit, hell, damn*— with proper punctuation—on a wall."

Stunned, Zora felt her eyes widen and a shocked laugh burst from her throat. She shot him a look. "Princess?" she asked skeptically.

His gaze settled on hers, skimmed her face and brushed over her lips, causing her to heat up in places that were already pretty damned stoked. "It fits. You're regal. Classy." He looked away and she caught the edge of his droll smile. "And you expect everyone to kiss your royal ass."

Zora stepped into the elevator, hit the button for their floor. She leaned heavily against the mirrored wall. "I don't expect anyone to kiss my ass," she said levelly, "however, I'm thinking about putting my foot up yours."

Where was his notebook? she wondered, vaguely noting that he didn't have it with him. He'd been taking copious notes again today and the one time she'd tried to peek over his shoulder, he'd competently shielded it from her view. Which made her all the more determined to know what he'd written. She'd also seen him on the phone, which had begged the question, who the hell was he talking to?

Tate laughed, sidled into her personal space and placed both his hands on the wall on either side of her head. Her pulse tripped. He was close enough that she caught his scent, something smooth and clean, and she could make out tiny dark brown flecks in his compelling amber eyes. Her belly clenched and a bolt of heat arrowed into her trembling womb.

"My point is," he remarked patiently, "as a result of your whole *Educate Tate Hatcher* mandate, I have been plagued, harangued, harassed and harped at all damned day."

From the throbbingly weary tone of his voice, you'd think he'd been sentenced to life in hell. Funny that she found that endearing.

"I have not had a single minute to myself— even to attend to personal matters," he added pointedly, "and, on the rare occasions I've been permitted to string two thoughts together, I've thought about— Here, I'll show you."

Before she could respond, Tate leaned forward and fastened his hungry mouth to hers. Zora was hit with the almost overwhelming urge to laugh, to weep. With relief, she supposed. She was giddy, an emotion she could confidently claim hadn't happened to her since she'd entered adulthood.

But Tate Hatcher—the last true bachelor and unwitting bane of her recent existence—had the limited ability to make her feel all sorts of things she wasn't accustomed to feeling. Made her feel things she wouldn't name or admit because doing so would make her vulnerable. Would concede power and, as long as she kept it to herself—just like all of her emotions—she remained the master of her person, the boss of her limited universe. She remained on top.

Zora sagged against him, wound her arms around his neck and returned his kiss with the same sort of mad, mindless hunger he was currently showing her. She'd thought about him all day. Her gaze had been inexplicably drawn to him. She could feel him, *feel* his very presence pinging her like sonar.

The memory of last night had been her constant companion, had kept her insides hot and melting, quivery and anxious. The taste of his kiss, the salty tang of his skin, the feel of his hot mouth latched onto her breast and the expert skill he'd showcased with those talented orgasm-provoking fingers.

It was more than mere sexual attraction. He was a fever, a disease, a shadow she couldn't shake—a beast, dammit—but for reasons she couldn't explain, that made him all the more appealing. She liked that he was a little rough around the edges, appreciated his honesty after being with so many mealy-mouthed, self-serving *liars*. There was no wondering what Tate thought, or what he might do. No jockeying for a better position, or pretensions.

The book was an issue, yes, but knowing what she knew now, Zora was finding it harder and harder to hold a grudge. Did she want him to see the light? To give her gender the respect it deserved? Definitely. A joke—as he insisted—or no, it was still harmful to their cause. But frankly, after learning about his mother, Zora didn't know whether he'd ever be able to completely let his anger go. To completely overcome the unflattering opinions he'd formed out of bitterness and self-preservation.

She'd wanted to reform him for Chicks-In-Charge, then to fix him because he was wrong. But her agenda had taken a new turn. Now she wanted to fix him because he ached. Because beneath all the bullshit bravado, he was still waiting for the milk for his cereal. Still waiting to be lovable.

Tate sucked her tongue into his mouth, slipped his fingers beneath the waistband of her pants and drew little circles in the small of her back with the pads of his thumbs. Her nipples tingled and pearled, puckered beneath her bra for his kiss, and warmth seeped into her panties. She refused to call what she was feeling love, but didn't mind using the term in another context.

She pulled her mouth from his. "I don't want to play poker."

He kissed the side of her mouth. "I made up some new rules. This is dirty poker, with customized chips."

Zora pushed her fingers into his hair and tasted the steady beat at the hollow of his throat. "Sounds intriguing, however, I just want you to make love to me."

A hiss whistled between his teeth as she bit lightly on his neck. "Well, hell, I was going to do that anyway." A definite, mouthwatering bulge rocked suggestively against her belly, making her entire body erupt in gooseflesh.

"Do it faster."

Tate kissed her again as the elevator slid to a smooth stop and Zora was only vaguely aware of the doors opening.

She immediately became aware of something else, though—they weren't alone. Frankie, Carrie and April stood framed in the metal doorway.

"She'd said stick to him like glue," April remarked drolly, "but I had no idea that she meant it literally."

Carrie gaped. "Talk about sleeping with the enemy."

Tate sent her a glance, snugged her up closer to his side. "What? Aren't you going to introduce me to the family?"

"They know who you are," Zora said, trying hard not to squirm. She'd confided in Frankie, but hadn't had a chance to speak with the other two yet. At least, not about the personal turn her and Tate's relationship had taken. Frankie had obviously thought they'd take it better coming from her, but it probably would have been to her advantage if they hadn't just caught her with Tate's tongue down her throat and his hands in her pants. "And you know who they are, so introductions aren't necessary."

Tate nudged her forward out of the elevator, then held the door open for her friends. He smiled. "I believe ya'll were going down?"

"Yeah, but I think—"

Frankie nudged April forward, causing her to utter a startled oomph. "We'll all get together and talk later," Frankie finished smoothly, herding them into the waiting elevator. She shot Zora a meaningful look. "Breakfast?"

Zora nodded. "I'll see you then."

April frowned and her mouth worked like a fish out of water. "But, I don't understand. Just last week she said he was a rotten bottom-feeding bas—" Thankfully, the doors slid closed before she could finish the rest of that sentence.

"You didn't tell them you want me?" Tate teased. His smile was a bit uncertain and though she couldn't be sure, she thought she detected the slightest hint of disappointment in his voice.

"I'd told Frankie," Zora said, searching his face for hidden clues to his thoughts. "But I haven't had a chance to bring it up to April and Carrie yet." She hesitated, grimaced. "Frankie's not thrilled—any more than any of your friends would be about me, I imagine—but at least she understands."

His brow furrowed. "Understands what?"

Zora fisted her hands in his shirt and jerked him to her for a long, slow, mind-numbing kiss. "Sexual attraction. Animal drive."

She felt him smile against her lips. "Are you saying you want to use me for my body?"

"I'm looking for your brain," she deadpanned. "By all accounts, it's between your legs."

"Smartass."

She cocked her head. "Better than being a dumbass. You'll have to tell me what it feels like."

Tate fished his key out of his pocket and inserted it into the lock. "What what feels like?"

"Being plugged into a genius."

He shot her a puzzled look. "Being plugged into a gen—" His eyes widened. "Oh, hell," he sighed, evidently realizing he'd walked right into that one. He put his hand on the back of her neck and gave her a gentle nudge into his room. "New rule, princess. Your vocabulary just sank to six words—*yes, harder, faster, please, thank* and *you.*"

Zora chuckled. "I'll try to remember that."

He closed the door behind them and cupped her face in his hands, kissed her until her skin burned, her belly shook and every cell in her body sang with needy anticipation. He pulled back and his whiskey gaze tangled with hers. "Try real hard."

8

TATE HATCHER HAD LOST his virginity at fourteen
when one of the ladies he cut grass for had invited
him in for a cold drink on a particularly hot afternoon. She'd been a hot older woman—in her
mid-twenties—and he'd been a taller-than-aver-
age boy with ripening hormones and the intense
urge to dip his wick.

Since then he'd been getting laid on a regular
basis and was confident of his abilities to pleasure
a woman. Since meeting Zora in person he'd been
consumed with the idea of landing between her
legs, and truth be told, he'd thought about it be-
forehand, as well. Had dreamed about it, ob-
sessed over various ways to put that lush mouth
to better, more pleasurable use. He realized now
that he'd been drawn to her even then, that some
part of him recognized some part of her. Fate?
Karma? Hell, who knew. He certainly didn't.

But since coming here, he'd been able to think
of little else, and yet now that the time was at

hand, he was suddenly afraid he'd fall short of the mark, terrified he'd disappoint her. Logically, he knew better. Hell, she hadn't had sex in months he knew, suspected even longer. He'd pulled an orgasm from her in under thirty seconds last night.

And yet, Tate instinctively knew—and instinctively resisted—that being with Zora Anderson was going to be different. Making love to her would be special because she called to him on so many different levels. He'd noticed things about her that he'd never noticed about other women. That Little Dipper freckle pattern on her nose, for instance, or the way her hair had a tendency to fall over her left eye when it wasn't pulled back.

He'd noticed today that she ate her food one serving at a time, finished it completely before moving on to the next item on the dish. Broccoli, turned the plate. Steamed squash, turned the plate. Grilled chicken, turned the plate. He thought it was cute. Cute, dammit. Adorable and endearing. How screwed up was that? He shouldn't be staring at her long enough to note these things, much less feel a warm little rush in his chest once he did. He should be thinking about nothing beyond taking her to bed, feeling her hot body gloving him, or the slide of her tongue down the side of his neck.

But for the first time since he'd gotten to the hotel, Tate was aware of the end of the conference—the end of their time together. Tomorrow after lunch, the festivities would officially wrap up and then what would happen to them? The idea of never seeing her again, of never listening to that sweet, sultry voice, or missing an opportunity to rattle her—shake that steely resolve— made a cold hard knot of dread form in his belly. The idea of never kissing her again—just kissing her—made him break out in a cold sweat.

He didn't know what to do, and honestly he was torn between trying to find a way to prevent all of the above from happening, and being angry at her for making him worry about it in the first place. Though it galled him to no end, he was having to sort out *feelings*. Quite honestly, he wasn't used to feeling any true emotions at all— the superficial ones were easy. He didn't have to invest anything of himself.

But whether he liked it or not—for better or for worse—he found himself invested in her. Reluctantly, thrillingly invested in her. And tonight, he fully intended to make her reciprocate the gesture.

Tomorrow couldn't be the end.

Tonight couldn't be it.

And he had absolutely no intention of writing another book that purposely or inadvertently belittled her cause. To hell with his notes, with Blake, with the damned book. Aside from wanting his life back, his heart simply wasn't in it. Not anymore. Oh, he taken a few notes, made a few uncharitable insights, particularly the first day. Out of spite more than anything and because he'd had Blake pestering the piss out of him. But listening to these women—listening to her, in particular— had made him face some hard truths about himself and the book he'd written. Yes, it had for the most part been a joke, but it had been hurtful, had unintentionally exacerbated a real problem.

Seeing all these women band together, listening to them actively trying to help each other—hell, she'd had workshops on everything from financial management to how to change a tire—had given his prerogative a significant adjustment. He'd rather be gutted with a butter knife than admit it, but it had. But knowing and admitting were two completely different things. Admitting meant he'd have to admit he was wrong, an unnatural phrase for him. In fact, he didn't think he'd ever said it.

Furthermore, more than anything, he wanted to know what had happened to her—what had made her start Chicks-In-Charge. He'd been appalled to hear a portion of Frankie's story and intuitively knew that Zora's was just as bad, if not worse. He was determined to get it out of her, to make her tell him. He needed to know. If he didn't know, then he couldn't help. And, whether she knew it or not, she desperately needed it.

Tate turned her to face him, searched those light green eyes with his and allowed her to see a part of the turmoil currently tearing him up. The desire and uncertainty, the heat and the fear and that tender emotion he dared not name. He traced a comma down the side of her cheek, almost staggered from the impact. *Defend, nurture, dominate, protect.* "You win, princess. I'm not writing another book like the first one." That's it, that's all he could concede right now. Couldn't elaborate. Luckily, he watched the knowledge penetrate that keen mind, watched it slowly bloom in a smile across her lips, and he didn't have to.

She understood.

Tate let go a relieved breath, then ever so gently, ever so reverently, framed her face and lowered his mouth to hers.

For the first time in his misbegotten life, Tate intended to make love to a woman. Not just have sex, pleasure or screw.

Make love…and in some bizarre way, it was like being a virgin all over again.

ZORA INSTANTLY MARKED the change in him, glimpsed a bit of the feelings working on him right now. Those aged-whiskey eyes were awash in uncertainty, desire, affection and confusion, and it tore at her heart because she felt them as well. She didn't want to, didn't need to, but was past caring about anything outside this moment. Furthermore, she knew she only saw them because he allowed her to, and for some reason, the small concession from her arrogant beast melted her heart like butter over a hot bun.

You win, princess… Sweeter words had never been spoken. They'd done it. They'd gotten through to him. She'd never doubted his word—never doubted that he'd use any of her personal information against her. He was unfailingly honest and in that regard, though it might not have been wise, she'd trusted him. A complete turnaround—much less a small confession—was more than she could have hoped for, and yet her macho monster had managed to do both.

For her, she instinctively knew, and nothing had ever touched her more.

The trembling brush of his fingers snatched the breath from her lungs, but he swiftly lowered his mouth and breathed more back in. The kiss was slow and soft, deliberate and drugging. It wound through her limbs like warm molasses, sluggish and smooth, and her belly vibrated with a combination of fear and need.

She stood on the edge of the point of no return, knew that after this night with Tate she'd never be the same. It was more than lust, more than affection. It was that terrifying, unnamed emotion, the one that misted her eyes and made her throat tight.

It was a poor time to realize she was in love, but she couldn't do anything about it, any more than she could stop what they'd started. He was currently pulling the pins out of her hair, letting it down one section at a time, and she felt the tumblers in her heart slip into place as each pin fell unheeded to the floor. By the time the final pin dropped from his hand, she was firmly, desperately, unwisely, miserably in love.

With Tate Hatcher, her archenemy.

Tate's hands roamed slowly down her back, molded her more firmly to him. She felt a prominent nudge prod her belly and that simple touch caused a rush of warmth to coat her folds. Lust licked her veins and a year of abstinence—of erotic neglect—swept over her like a riptide, pulling her under, making her desperate. Slow was wonderful and she appreciated a man who knew how to take his time, but right now Zora wasn't interested in a grand seduction—she wanted to multitask.

She upped the tempo of their kiss and tugged

the shirt from the waistband of his pants. Tate groaned into her mouth, and she savored that masculine sigh, wanted to eat more of them. Eat *him*. Lave his nipples, nip his shoulder, taste every glorious inch of him, particularly that soft, smooth skin encasing the hardest part of him.

Emboldened, Zora pushed her hands up over his back, mapped muscle and measured bone. It wasn't enough. She set to work on the buttons on his shirt, freed the last one, and with a sigh of sheer delight, pushed the garment off his shoulders. Tate finished shrugging out of it, then did the same with hers. He bent and kissed each new part of skin he revealed, slipped his tongue over the mounds of her breasts. Her knees quaked, her thighs burned. Another barb of heat twisted in her womb, made her all the more desperate to have him fill her up and obliterate the achy hollow feeling currently building between her legs.

She had to have him. Now.

Zora backed him toward the bed and gave him a gentle push. He landed on the mattress with a soft oomph. "You should get naked," she suggested, calmly shedding her bra.

Tate chuckled, his eyes darkened and his hands instantly went to the button on his trousers. "Those words aren't in the vocabulary I gave you." He shucked his pants and briefs in one fell swoop, kicked them aside. "Now I'll have to punish you."

Zora's gaze dropped below his waist and the impressive sight that greeted her hungry gaze made her mouth alternately parch and water. He was... *Oh. My. God.* She slid her own pants and undies over her hips and left them in a discarded, forgotten pile next to his.

Tate grabbed her around the waist, pulled her to him and instantly sucked her achy peak into his hot mouth. She gasped, squirmed and pressed her thighs together, a vain attempt to stem the flood of desire flowing steadily into her sex. One hand came up and kneaded the other breast, lest it feel neglected and she anchored her hands on his shoulders to remain upright. Her legs would scarcely support her. He sucked, he nipped, and with every skilled sweep of his tongue, her clit issued a resulting throb.

As if reading her mind, Tate tugged her onto the bed with him, and the first full-bodied flesh-to-flesh contact almost made her come. He felt beyond wonderful. He was hard and soft, big and thrilling. She loved the feel of her nipples against his chest, the feel of his masculine legs tangled with her smooth ones. The texture of his skin, his scent.

Everything.

Everything about him. She'd never in her life been so wild for a guy, so desperate to put one between her thighs. So drugged and mindless. The entire hotel could come crumbling down around them and so long as she was tangled in his embrace, she honestly wouldn't care. So long as the promise of his body fitting to hers remained, she'd gladly pay any price.

Zora rolled him onto his back and worked her way down his chest with little licks and kisses, a playful bite. She couldn't taste or feel enough of him. She sucked at his male nipple, let her hand drift slowly over his belly, then took him in hand. He jerked against her palm, sucked a pleasurable hiss between clenched teeth. She worked the slippery skin over the impressive length of him, ran the pad of her thumb over the sensitive head and caught a pearl of his desire. She smiled against his belly, circled his navel with her tongue.

He knew what was coming and had braced himself. His thighs were locked and a broken chuckle bubbled up his arched throat. "Zora, you're killing me."

She bent down and sucked the whole of him into her mouth. He gasped, bucked, groaned in sexual agony. "Thank you."

She ate him once more, pulled him deep into her mouth and worked her tongue against him.

Hard flicks, soft licks and every variation in between. She fondled him, sucked hard and worked him up and down, up and down until she could taste beginning climax, the salty evidence of his desire. But she didn't want him to come, at least not yet. When he came she wanted him to be inside her, she wanted to feel every ridge, vein and tremor, wanted to absorb them into her own body, then give them back again through hers.

"Zora," he said warningly.

She smiled, caught his gaze, then lazily licked the engorged head once more. "Hand me a condom, would you?" she asked.

Tate snagged one from the nightstand, where evidently he'd placed them earlier, and handed it to her. Zora tore into it with her teeth, fished it out and then swiftly rolled it into place.

Then she straddled him, felt her trembling sex ride the ridge of his arousal. Her eyes drifted shut under the weight of the exquisite sensation. His hard to her soft. After a moment, she looked down and the picture he made in that moment would be indelibly imprinted on her brain. Six and half feet of hard, handsome male. Smooth muscle, gleaming skin. Eyes dark and slumberous and a mouth curled into one of the sexiest grins she'd ever had the pleasure to see. His hair was mussed—which was nothing new—but seeing that dark head lying submissively on a pillow was not something one saw every day.

And, as it turned out, it was not something she was going to enjoy anymore. Without warning, Tate easily flipped her. Initially, Zora panicked. She couldn't set the pace, couldn't control the outcome. Couldn't move. It terrified her. After the dugout incident, she'd never let a guy on top of her, had always maintained the dominant position—she'd never lain flat on her back. Had been flat against the wall, maybe, or backed up against the shower, but in bed *she* was the one on top.

She conjured a smile, terrified that he'd see her fear, and attempted to roll him back over. She might as well be trying to move Mount Rushmore with a spoon. The hard length of him glided between her folds, nudged her clit. Zora gasped, instinctively arched beneath him. She whimpered. God, she was so close. Wanted it so bad.

Tate tilted her chin, forcing her to look into his eyes. "Let me, Zora," he whispered. "I won't let you down."

He knew, she realized. How, she couldn't imagine. But he did. She swallowed her fear, but not her pride. "You've got ninety seconds."

Those whiskey eyes widened with admiration and he laughed. "I can do it in ten if you want me to." He rocked against her once more, making her breath stutter out in uneven gasps.

Zora pushed up against him, gripped the twin muscles of his ass. "I don't care, so long as you can do it again."

Tate's soft laugh resonated with masculine confidence. "Princess, that won't be a problem."

And with that loaded remark, he drew back and plunged into her.

Zora's mouth opened in a harsh gasp. Spots danced before her eyes, the room swelled and then shrank back into focus. He was hot, hard and huge, and he filled her completely, pushed out every bit of ache and loneliness in her womb and chest. She clenched her feminine muscles around him, imprisoning him there until her world shifted back to rights. It was pain and pleasure combined, the ultimate sensation, and if she hadn't been in love with him before, she was hopelessly head over heels now. Her heart ached with joy even while her belly trembled with need. Zora looked up and caught him staring at her, caught that same unguarded look that told her he, too, was deeply affected.

He bent down and brushed his lips over hers, a promise, an entreaty, and she responded in kind, giving him herself as well. He began to move inside her, slowly at first, but steady, and matched his thrusts to the erotic play in their mouths. She sucked at his tongue, clamped around him, could feel the tension building and building until she was wild with lust, blinded by need. She tore her mouth from his, leaned up and licked the hollow of his throat, gripped his ass more firmly beneath her hands and urged him on. His breath came in short puffs, his masculine sounds of pleasure music to her ears. He plowed in and out of her.

"*Oh, yes,*" she cried. "*Harder, faster, please, thank you,*" she wailed, as the first quickening of beginning climax ripened in her sex. Her body absorbed the thrusts, relished the delicious friction, the different position. She whimpered, thrashed and bucked beneath him. "Oh, Tate. God— I need— Please, oh please," she begged shamelessly. She could feel it coming, could feel the tension preparing to snap. He bent his head, sucked her nipple deep into his mouth, then reached down between their joined bodies and thumbed her clit.

She fractured.

Her body arched off the bed, her neck bowed and her mouth opened in a long, soundless scream of satisfaction. Fireworks danced behind her closed lids, her body trembled from head to toe. She quaked, she burned, she fell apart. Her limbs liquefied and she spasmed hard around him, creating little lingering sparkles of pleasure deep in her womb.

A second later, Tate joined her. He pumped frantically, once, twice, three times. His lips curled back from his teeth, veins stuck out on his neck and every muscle in his body atrophied with pleasure. He buried himself to the hilt, planted himself as deeply into her body as he could and didn't move again. She literally felt the orgasm flash through him, felt a pulse of heat pool deep inside where it gathered at the end of the condom. The sensation caused another tremor in her, and he winced as she fisted around his sensitive shaft once more.

Tate's gaze held a twinkling quality when it found hers next and he bent and pressed another lingering kiss to her lips once more. Impossibly, she felt him swell within her once more.

"Hand me another condom, princess," he told her, his voice a deep, sexy rumble. "We're just getting started."

Zora grinned and happily obliged. A man of his word, she thought, now *that* was damned sexy.

9

TATE HAD ABSOLUTELY NO IDEA what time it was, but
he knew it had to be getting close to time for Zora
to report for her breakfast with the Chicks. The
heavy drapes competently blocked out the light,
but he could tell from the waking sounds of doors
opening and closing up and down the hall, and
from the beginning hum of Sunday morning traf-
fic, that dawn had come and gone, and morning
was fully upon them.

The musky aroma of sex hung in the air along
with Zora's particularly distinct scent—something sweet and cool, reminiscent of mint and
lilies. He'd asked her about it last night and she'd
told him that it was a custom fragrance, one of her
indulgences. She'd had various bath soaps, lo-
tions and oils made up of the stuff so that the
scents were layered and lingering. He could
vouch for that, Tate thought with a somewhat
tired smile. He smelled it in her hair, behind the
backs of her knees, even down to her little toes,

and he knew if he lived to be one hundred, he'd remember it for the rest of his life.

Last night when he'd slid into her—when he'd pushed himself into her and joined their bodies—that he-man sensation had absolutely permeated every cell, every pore, changed his very body chemistry and ultimately captured his heart.

She completed him.

The parts that he'd been missing? Well, he'd found them last night. Tate ordinarily didn't wax poetic, had never once entertained the idea that those men he'd ridiculed—that he'd called "whipped"—were hopelessly helpless against truly falling in love. It was the ultimate form of irony, the ultimate form of punishment.

But he got it now.

Understood why men were uncomfortable when their wives were angry. Why they bent over backward to make them happy. He swallowed, once again blinded by the sad, haggard image of his father. Even why some men went a little crazy when their wives left.

Tate didn't understand now any more than he ever had why his mother had walked out, but at least he understood a little of what had made his father miserable those last couple of years. The idea of losing Zora—whom he'd only just met—flat out terrified him.

He hated it. Hated that feeling of helplessness, of being out of control. Hated that by falling in love with her, he'd unwittingly handed her the power to hurt him. He'd sworn to himself—and vocally to others, including the entire United States—that *he'd* never dangle on the end of some woman's hook and yet here he was. He'd swallowed the whole damned thing, hook, line and sinker and she might as well have him preserved and mounted on a plaque on the wall. She was that stuck with him.

Tate imagined he would have fallen in love with her anyway, but what had really sent him over the edge was the fact that she'd let him take the lead role in their lovemaking. Though she'd tried to mask her initial panic with a smile, had tried to roll him back over and dominate, she'd ultimately opened her heart—and her trust—and let him love her. Afterward, during one of the few breaks they'd taken from making love, she'd told him about the dugout incident, how she'd never let a guy get on top of her again. Tate had been hit with the simultaneous urge to find the little bastard who'd frightened her and beat the living hell out of him, and to preen because being with him last night had resulted in a first for her as well.

That she cared about him enough to give him that trust—when he knew how fiercely she'd guarded it—had made Tate feel like he could conquer the world. He couldn't explain it, couldn't wrap his brain around it, but it didn't matter because a gesture like that spoke to the heart.

In short, it had changed him.

As soon as she woke up, he planned to talk to her about their relationship, to figure out some way to tell her that he wanted her around on a permanent basis. Without losing face, of course. He'd given up enough, he thought with a faint smile. Holding on to a little self-respect when she owned his heart didn't seem like too much to ask. He absently stroked her upper arm and a flutter of warmth ballooned in his chest. God, she was gorgeous. So heartbreakingly beautiful.

Zora stirred beside him. She didn't open her eyes, but that ripe, lush mouth curled into a feline grin and she stretched like a well-rubbed cat. *Against him*, which instantly summoned a note of approval from his dick. It stirred as well, ready for action.

She blinked sleepily. "*Yes, harder, faster, please, thank* and *you*," she said, that sultry voice lazy and rough from disuse.

Tate chuckled. "You're allowed to say other things now. We aren't making love."

She rolled over onto his chest, dipped her head into the hollow of his neck and nuzzled. Her nipples raked his chest, blazing trails of sensation and her wet sex settled firmly onto his, effectively pulling the breath from his lungs. "Says who?" she asked suggestively.

Tate grasped her hips, slid back and forth between her tender folds, making sure to bump her sweet spot. "You've got ninety seconds," he told her, throwing her words back at her.

She reached over, pulled the last condom from the nightstand and quickly sheathed him. She settled over him once more, then slowly, carefully, oh-so-deliberately sank down on top of him. Her lids fluttered shut and she smiled a soft, lazy, welcoming sort of smile. "I can do it in ten."

He flexed beneath her, pushed hard, chuckled. "I don't care, so long as you can do it again."

She leaned back farther. Her hair hung in flame-like curls over her creamy skin, brushed the tops of her breasts. Curvy hips, sweetly curved belly, wet red curls mingling with his darker ones where their bodies joined. If he'd ever seen anything more beautiful—more erotic—in his entire life he couldn't recall it.

"Baby," she said silkily. "*That* won't be a problem."

She pressed her hands down on his chest, lifted her hips. He felt her clamp around him, dragging his skin up creating the most fantastic sort of tension imaginable. Ten, hell, Tate thought. Another five seconds of that he was going to explode.

But he wasn't going to do it alone.

She rocked again, steadily rode him, up and down, up and down. Her skin flushed, her eyes drifted shut and her neck seemed too weak to support her head. Her breath came in jagged little puffs and she bit her lip, increased the tempo. He felt her quicken around him, felt her muscles tighten and quiver and, though it nearly killed him to master the concentration, Tate moved his hands around and pressed both his thumbs on either side of her clit.

She inhaled sharply, gasped and bucked desperately above him. She rode him hard—had mastered the art—and he met that frantic rhythm stroke for stroke. Tate gritted his teeth, felt his own loins ready for blastoff. Unable to hang on much longer, he pressed harder, thumbed her harder. "Yes, please, harder, faster, thank and you," he growled, pistoning in and out of her.

She fisted around him, came, and he erupted right along with her. Her breathing ragged, she sank down on top of him. Her hair fanned out over his chest, slid down and tickled his side. "God, that was…amazing," she said, her voice tired from the exertion.

Tate slid his fingers down the smooth slope of

her back, kissed her head. "No complaints here, that's for damned sure."

She reluctantly sat up, squinted at the clock. Her eyes widened. "I've got to go."

"I know," he said, carefully disentangling himself from her. "Why don't we save time and take a quick shower together? I want to talk to you."

Her eyes twinkled with humor. "You want to *talk.* In the *shower.*"

He chuckled. "I know it sounds like it can't be done, but I thought we'd give it a shot."

She stood and shrugged. "I'm game if you are."

By the time Zora returned with her soap and shampoo, Tate had adjusted the tap. He let her get in first, then followed her inside. She curled into his chest, pressed a kiss against his neck. Just hugged him, and the simple affectionate gesture made his throat clog with some nebulous obstruction. "What did you want to talk about?"

He drew back and looked down at her. "Us."

Her full poker mask didn't fall completely into place, but her gaze grew somewhat shuttered all the same. "Us?" she repeated. "What about us?"

"I want there to be an us."

"You mean beyond today?"

Tate nodded. "Beyond today, beyond tomorrow. Beyond…whenever. I've grown quite…fond of you." He knew he should tell her that he loved her, had fully intended to, but finding the courage when it came right down to it was just too damned hard. *He* was the chicken. But he'd given her as much as he could for the moment. She could read him, was counting on that keen perception now to ferret out the frightening truth. Tate held his breath, waited for her to respond.

WHEN TATE HAD SUGGESTED they talk, the very last thing Zora'd expected was *this*. She saw something in that whiskey gaze that she'd never expected to see, something that equally awed and terrified. He wasn't merely fond of her—she knew it. Like her, at some point over this weekend, between barbs, poker, revelations, laughs and making love, he'd fallen for her, too. And like her, he was too proud and too frightened to admit it. Which was fine, Zora thought, because she was no more comfortable admitting how she felt right now than he was.

She felt a trembling smile slide into place as she searched his gaze. "I've grown rather…fond of you, too."

He breathed an endearing, audible sigh of relief, bent down and kissed her nose. "Good."

"There are issues, though," Zora felt compelled to qualify, "that won't go away, no matter how much time we spend in bed. Between my friends, your friends and our outspoken views we've each shared in the media, it's going to be…difficult." Which was a vast understatement. It would be sheer hell. Particularly at first, and most especially for Tate.

"I'm aware of that, which is why I think that after you're done here today, you should come to my house tonight…and bring a toothbrush. We can work it all out. Get a game plan." He lifted one powerful shoulder in a lose shrug. "I'm going to be eating crow. I'll expect you to make it worth my while," he growled suggestively.

She laughed, considered him for a moment. "I don't think that'll be a problem." He needed more than that, Zora surmised. Not necessarily a promise, but at the very least a little assurance. After last night, he should have it, but she had the feeling until he was completely sure of her feelings for him, he was going to have to be told—shown—repeatedly, that he was lovable. She'd known this going in, hadn't she? That her beast had a tender, breakable heart.

"I'll give you my address before you go down to your breakfast." He chuckled grimly. "Be forewarned, those Chicks of yours are going to peck you to death. I don't think you're going to like it."

Zora had already thought of that, but thankfully she suspected that Frankie had done damage control last night. "I don't need your address—I know where you live. And they aren't going to peck me to death, dammit. They're concerned, Tate. There's a difference."

He stilled and a crafty smile turned his lips. "You had me checked out, didn't you?"

She nodded. "Of course."

"Well, before you start feeling too smug you should know I had you checked out as well. Nice landscaping, by the way. Who's your gardener?"

Zora laughed. She'd figured as much. They were startlingly alike to hold such different opinions. She reached for her shampoo. "Do you mind letting me get under there first?" she asked, gesturing toward the spray. "I've really got to hurry."

"No, go ahead. I'll soap up…and watch you."

She lathered her hair, tilted her head back and gasped when she felt his fingers brush her nipples. "Cut it out, beast. I don't have time."

"Beast?"

"That's right," she said, enjoying his attention all the same, the feel of that hot gaze on her body. She shook her head, changing the stream of the water in order to get the last of the soap from her hair. "But *my* beast."

"I kind of like the sound of that."

"Just as much as I like it when you kiss my royal ass."

He chuckled again, a sexy rumble, bent and pulled her nipple into his mouth. "Turn around and I'll kiss it right now," he murmured suggestively.

Zora sighed, tempted but unable. "Later," she promised. She straightened and moved to get out of the shower. "If I don't get a chance to see you after lunch, then I'll see you tonight."

He drew her back and kissed her soundly. "I'm fond of you," he repeated.

Her heart warmed and tingled. "I'm fond of you, too."

Zora quickly wrapped up in a towel and made her way back into the bedroom to gather her things. She could get her clothes later, but part of her makeup was in her purse. She was halfway across the room before Tate's confounded notebook caught her eye. It lay innocently on the dresser. Zora hesitated, tempted beyond reason and struggled with whether to peek or not. Before they'd become lovers, it had been a no-brainer, but now it seemed too much like an invasion of his privacy. Still, it wasn't like showing up at her conference—for research purposes, of all things—hadn't been an invasion of her privacy. It couldn't hurt anything. Right? Right. He had nothing to hide. Had told her he was an open book. Fine, then. She'd read.

Before she could change her mind, she snatched it up and flipped it open to the first page. Tate's masculine scrawl filled various parts of the page.

Great legs, great mouth. Both could be put to better use.

She giggled, she couldn't help herself. Her tactless beast, she thought fondly, as her idiotic heart did a little somersault.

God, she's gorgeous. Be even more gorgeous naked. This constant clucking is getting on my nerves!

Best workshop—learning how to change a tire. One less thing a guy has to do. How about one for changing the oil?

Zora chuckled. She'd been feeling all smug because he'd abandoned his book idea, but now she wasn't so sure if he'd let it go for her, or because he hadn't had anything better to work with than this. Still smiling, she closed the notebook, made her way to Tate's desk to pick up her purse. The surface was cluttered with his mobile office, a laptop, printer and fax. If she'd noticed that night before last, she would have saved herself a great deal of embarrassment, Zora thought with a wry smile. But then she wouldn't have had the privilege of seeing him wet and naked, so she supposed it was a wash.

She picked up her purse and was just about to

leave when a piece of paper with a familiar phrase caught her attention.

Chicks-In-Charge.

Zora stilled. Her heart rate jumped into overdrive and a sense of foreboding made her belly do a queasy figure eight. Why would anyone send Tate a fax about Chicks-In-Charge? she wondered. Unless... But no, she thought faintly.

Seemingly from far away, Zora watched her hand reach out and lift the fax from the tray. She started at the top with the date and time—last night at ten-twelve—then worked her way down. Funny that they hadn't heard it, but then they'd been otherwise occupied. They weren't quiet lovers. Zora read the brief message and by the time she'd finished it, every bit of the new-love euphoria had drained out of her and had been replaced with a cold, hard knot of fury.

Tate,
I met Cindy for drinks and went over what we'd discussed earlier today—the penis-envy hook. She loved it. Like me, was particularly intrigued by the fact that Zora Anderson could pee standing up. Gives a whole new meaning to the phrase penis envy, eh? Use it. You've got the go-ahead. Anything else you can dig up about her

would be helpful, too. Cindy gave you an
extra week on the proposal, but the deadline
for delivery of the complete is set in stone.
No wiggle room. Get to work.
Blake

The best Zora could figure out, Cindy was
Tate's editor and Blake evidently was his agent.
Though her mind was a mass of miserable angry
thoughts, Zora vaguely recalled them being mentioned on the acknowledgment page of his book.
Who they were, she knew, wasn't necessarily important—but what she'd just read was.

You win, princess…

Her eyes stung. She'd won something all
right—the Fool of the Year Award. She'd wrongfully assumed that, just because he'd been honest
about everything else, his word would be good,
too. Quite frankly that she'd been wrong simply
stunned her. She was normally pretty good at
spotting a fib, of discerning a shady character.
There'd been nothing hidden about Tate—he'd
shown her everything, had shared, she'd thought,
every feeling and wrongheaded idea in that stubborn, conceited, crafty noggin of his. That glib
honesty had been one of the things that she'd
liked about him, one of the things that had drawn
him to her in the beginning.

She'd given him complete access to her and to the conference, but with one condition—he couldn't use her personal information. Naturally, her biggest concern had been that he'd tell the world about Dex, that he'd make a fool out of her, thereby belittling her work in and for Chicks-In-Charge. That he'd told his agent about her unusual talent didn't bother her—her friends and family knew, it was a running joke of sorts—but it was the motivation behind the act—becoming unwilling—unwitting—book fodder was absolutely intolerable. *Penis envy, my ass,* Zora thought, her irritation overriding the initial breaking of her heart.

She'd be damned before she'd become his "hook."

She was seething, literally seething. Her hands shook, her cheeks stung. Even her eyeballs were hot. She wasn't just angry, not merely mad—she was friggin' *pissed.*

Clearly she'd been wrong. She couldn't fix him. He was too far gone, damaged beyond repair.

He chose that unfortunate moment to walk out of the bathroom. Zora looked up and pinned him with a venomous gaze. Tate's stepped slowed and the towel he'd been drying his hair with stilled. His gaze bounced from her face to the fax. "What's that?" he asked warily.

"This is a fax from your agent," Zora managed to say through clenched teeth. "You can read it yourself. From hell," she added, shoving it at him as she walked past.

"Zora," Tate called, baffled. "Wait. I—"

Zora spun around. She knew she shouldn't linger, knew that getting away from him was the best possible thing she could do. Knew that telling him even a fraction of what was on her mind would undoubtedly wind up in his damned book, but something simply just came over her. She just snapped, went ballistic and let fly.

"You bastard," she snarled. "I can't believe you! I can't believe that you've been here this entire weekend and that you still don't get it." Her voice climbed and her hands shook, but her capacity to harbor pain had reached its end and she was going to erupt. "How could you be here this weekend, listen to these women, see what we're about—not to mention screw me in the literal sense—and still write that damned book? Penis envy?" she all but screeched. "I asked one thing of you—just one," she clarified. "And that was this—keep my private life private. Don't use any of my personal information." Her eyes widened. "And that's your damned hook?"

He blinked, taken aback, then swore. His gaze

flew to the fax and his face became a thunder-cloud of irritation. "Zora, if you'll just give me a—"

"No, I'm not going to give you another damned thing," Zora countered. She'd given him enough. Her body, her heart, her trust—all of which had been misplaced. Her heart was break-ing, but being able to finally let go of years of anger and irritation felt too damned good to stop. "You wanted to know why I started Chicks-In-Charge? Well I'm going to tell you. Chicks-In-Charge was born on the same day I got dumped and fired by someone I mistakenly thought loved me. I made the dubious mistake of getting in-volved with my boss, then helping him build up a company. *Guy Talk?*" she said, smirking. "Ever heard of it?"

Other than a brief nod, he stood completely still, as though any false move would make her attack.

"Once I'd helped triple circulation, helped pull the magazine out of the red, my boyfriend/boss decided it was inconvenient to have me around, particularly since he'd started sleeping with one of the copy editors."

It didn't hurt now like it had then, but now she had a much worse pain to deal with—losing what might have been with Tate. Zora tried to blink back tears, tried to swallow past the lump in her throat. Tried…and failed.

Which made her all the more angry.

She smiled bitterly. "I know that you're not going to care—my opinion's about as good as your word is to you—but I'm going to say it, anyway." She dashed a tear off her cheek, cleared her throat. Hated that he'd seen her this way. It would have been so much better if she could've acted like she didn't care. But that was an old role she'd grown weary of playing, and conjuring the artifice was simply beyond her at this point. "I expected better of you. I didn't always like what you thought, or what you said, but I could usually figure out just what was going on in that head of yours. You're unfailingly—tactlessly—honest. It was part of your charm." She gestured toward the fax. Her throat constricted painfully. "But I didn't expect this. I didn't expect you to lie. Guess I got that one wrong, eh?"

Zora snatched her purse, her clothes, cursed the smell of their lovemaking and the time she'd spent in his bed. God, she'd been such a fool. Such a pathetic fool.

"Zora, wait. You don't understand. I'm not writing the damned book. I told you so last night. I—"

"Go to hell, Tate," she said wearily, completely

spent. "Shove your *special book* up your *special ass*." And without sparing him a backward glance, she retreated to her room, closed the door and purposely fitted the lock into place.

Thankfully, the sound disguised the breaking of her heart.

10

TATE FLINCHED AS SHE SLAMMED the door, struggled with the incongruity of what had just happened. He'd wanted to break that steely reserve, to shake her up, to make her tip her emotional hand. That had been one of his goals and, from the shocking display of anger he'd just witnessed, he'd definitely accomplished that.

He wished now he hadn't.

Tate had known that the impetus behind her forming Chicks-In-Charge had to be something big, knew that after hearing Frankie's story that Zora's had to be just as bad, if not worse. What he hadn't expected upon learning that some asshole had capitalized on that brilliant, crafty mind, had had the privilege of sharing that gorgeous body, then had dumped and fired her in one fell swoop, was the almost overpowering urge to track the guy down and pummel the hell out of him. Then jerk him up by the scruff of the neck and make him apologize. Tate's numb hands involuntarily formed fists.

Unfortunately, that would have to come later because right now he had to figure out a way to let her know that he hadn't been lying—honestly, it seemed like she could have given him the benefit of the doubt. Then again, he supposed she'd done that by trusting his word to start with. Still, that she'd flown completely off the handle without giving him so much as a chance for rebuttal irritated the hell out of him. He'd told her that he wasn't writing the damned book. He'd meant it. She meant more, what she was doing through Chicks-In-Charge was far more important than padding his pockets. In fact, getting out of the contract for the second book was going to seriously reduce the ready cash in his pockets.

He glanced at the fax again, briefly entertained the idea of throttling Blake. He could see where Zora could easily reach the conclusion that he'd lied to her. Could easily see why she'd be hurt and angry. The image of her tear-stained face loomed instantly to mind, causing an uncomfortable sensation to writhe in his belly. The fact that she'd been so hurt that she'd cried trumped his righteous indignation, and the idea that he might actually lose her surfaced in his muddled brain.

She'd lost it. Freaked. Then she'd cried.

Oh, hell, Tate thought. If he didn't fix this right now—if he gave her even an hour to think about what had happened—she'd shut him out. Cut him off. He knew it.

Tate calmly resumed getting ready, studiously ignored the helpless sense of panic crowding into his heart and chest. He would not entertain the idea that she wouldn't listen to him, that she wouldn't be with him. Wouldn't be... *fond* of him anymore.

She was mad, and rightly so, but he could fix this, he told himself. He would have to humble himself, apologize even though he hadn't really done anything wrong, then he'd have to beg for forgiveness. Again, even though he wasn't technically at fault. All the things that he was fundamentally opposed to, all the things that he'd sworn he would never do. Did he look forward to it? No, he dreaded it like hell. But there were no words for the horror of losing her—and he'd *do* anything, *say* anything to keep that from happening.

Ideally talking to his chick alone would be best, but he knew she'd never allow it. So he'd just have to corner her in the henhouse.

"THAT BASTARD!"

"Son of a bitch."

"Asshole."

Zora managed a watery grin. Nothing like a little group friend therapy. Initially she'd planned on keeping it to herself, not letting them know what had happened—it was too damned humiliating to admit she'd be so unforgivably stupid—but Frankie had taken one look at her red-rimmed eyes and demanded details.

Before she realized what was happening, Zora had broken down and sobbed—she'd never *sobbed* over anything in her life, which had made her cry harder—and the next instant she'd been gathered up in a group hug and they were all threatening everything from Tate Hatcher's life to dismemberment of his private organs.

"I never liked him," April said.

"Me, either," Carrie concurred.

They both turned to Frankie, shot her a reproachful look when she didn't readily jump onto the bash boat. Frankie studied Zora. "I'm reserving judgment," she said thoughtfully. "I don't think this is over yet."

Zora snorted, dabbed her eyes. "Trust me. It's over." Her heart issued another pitiful wail. Good grief, after a lifetime of guarding emotions and being able to hold back tears, she couldn't believe that she'd just *exploded* like that.

Granted it had felt wonderful, if a bit unexpected and out of control. But in all honesty, she should have expected it. Every feeling she'd had pertaining to Tate Hatcher had been exaggerated, bigger and more intense. Now that she'd had a chance to calm down, it was hardly surprising that being mad at him—hurt by him—would be any different.

Frankie hesitated, shot her a look. "Look, I know this is the last thing you want to hear, but—"

Zora glared at her. "Frankie, I love you like a sister, but if you say I told you so, I swear we'll tie up like a couple of rednecks over the last bag of pork rinds at the Pinch-A-Penny."

Frankie blinked. "I wasn't going say I told you so, dammit. I was going to suggest that one of us talk to him and try to do damage control. Penis envy," she snorted derisively. "He's really grasping at straws, isn't he?"

"Yeah, Zora," Carrie chimed in. "Being able to pee standing up is a cool trick, don't get me wrong. I'm envious. But I honestly don't see how he planned to write an entire book about it."

April nodded. "It's a pretty thin premise." Her sympathetic gaze found Zora's. "But I can see where you'd be hurt." She winced. "So he'd told you last night that he wasn't doing the book at all? That you'd won?"

Zora nodded and her throat closed. She just didn't get it. He'd seemed so tortured, so sincere.

How could she have read him so completely wrong? "That's right," she finally managed to say.

"And you found the fax this morning?" Carrie asked. "After you'd spent the night?"

She grunted bitterly. "Right again."

Frankie leaned back in her chair, seemed particularly thoughtful. "Is there any chance that he just hadn't told his agent yet? That he'd told you first?"

Actually, Zora had wondered that as well, but had deemed it wishful thinking. She couldn't imagine that being the case, but she supposed it wasn't out of the realm of possibility. Zora told her as much, shook her head. "I just don't think so."

Frankie hummed under her breath. "I don't know. Like I said, I'm reserving judgment. You know I thought this was a bad idea at the beginning, but I've been watching him, Zora. Watching *him* watch *you*," she said meaningfully. "And, for all of his faults, I didn't think being a liar was one of them. I think he's crazy about you." She snorted. "Last true bachelor my ass. He wants you." Frankie leaned down and snagged her purse. "We need to get in the banquet hall. Hard to believe that the conference is nearly over." She continued in that vein, as though the issue of Tate and Zora's broken heart had been settled and merited no further conversation.

Zora blindly reached down for her purse. *It's obvious he's crazy about you.* Could she have been that wrong? she wondered hesitantly. Could she have made such a huge mistake? Could he have been telling the truth? Was she so caught up in all men being faithless, dick-driven bastards that her perspective was that off the mark?

Until just a moment ago, she would have vehemently denied the accusation. But Frankie had made some excellent points. Zora's head throbbed, her heart ached and the possibility that she might have been wrong made her feel marginally better. Nevertheless, the possibility that she was right kept her aching head on straight. She just wanted to wrap this up, go home, lick her wounds and sort this mess out in private. She was weary and exhausted. Spent. It was too much to take in, too much to handle.

Her beast was being beastly.

"THANKS SO MUCH FOR ATTENDING our very first conference," Zora told the room at large, making her last public address of the day. "We hope that you walk away armed with new knowledge and the desire to better yourselves. To help each other. Several of you have come up to me and shared your enthusiasm for this group, for the Chicks-In-Charge organization, and for that on behalf of myself and the board, we thank you. We—" Zora drew up short as a murmur moved through the crowd and in the next instant she knew what had caused the stir—Tate. Her heart skipped a beat, raced and every ounce of moisture evaporated from her mouth. God, why couldn't he have just left? Did he have to hang around and make her miserable?

Tate looked up and caught her gaze, held up a finger and continued toward the front of the room. "I, uh—" He wound through the tables. "I know that you're wrapping things up here, but I thought since I was your *special guest*, you might let me make a little speech."

A little speech, Zora thought. She regarded him shrewdly. Just what was his angle? She looked to the board. "Any objections?" she asked.

They all shook their heads, the traitors.

Zora shrugged. "Sure," she relented, albeit reluctantly.

Looking curiously nervous—and a little grim— Tate came around and joined her behind the podium. He smiled at her, and she felt his gaze caress her face, note the fact that her eyes were still somewhat red and swollen. For a moment, she thought he was going to touch her cheek—his hand had drifted toward her—but he let it drop, apparently unsure of how she'd react to the gesture.

He stepped up to the microphone. "By now you all know who I am. You've all followed me around, talked to me." He chuckled. "Some of you even followed me into the bathroom." This comment drew a laugh from the crowd and a reluctant smile from Zora. "You were given the task of 'educating' me," Tate said with a significant look at Zora. "And I just wanted to let you know that you've succeeded." She heard him grind his teeth, watched his jaw work. "I was wrong."

Whoops of laughter and applause met that remark and Zora found herself uncomfortably stunned. Tate? Admitting fault? It was completely out of character and looked particularly painful.

"When I wrote my first book, I had no idea what women really want—and like most men, I seriously doubt that I'll ever figure it out. But as it happens, I'm not interested in knowing what *all* women want—" His gaze drifted to Zora and the depth of emotion in those whiskey eyes and the tentative smile on those gorgeous lips made her pulse zoom into warp speed, made her eyes mist with emotion. "I'm just interested in knowing what *that one* wants," he said gesturing to Zora. "I came here with the intent of gathering information for another book. My agent has called, e-mailed, faxed me," he said meaningfully, "the entire time that I've been here. 'What's your angle?' he's asked.

'Have you found a hook?' I mentioned in passing a curious little tidbit that Zora shared with me, one that fascinated me, and he took the idea and morphed it into the topic for my next book. The one, incidentally, I'd decided that I couldn't write." His gaze slid to Zora, then back to the room at large. "Thanks so much for 'educating' me," Tate said with a rueful smile. "It's, uh, it's been an experience."

The room broke into delighted applause and he even managed to get a standing ovation. Tate stepped back, leaned closer to her. "I told you last night that I wasn't going to write the damned book. There's another fax waiting on you in your room to prove it. If I wasn't so immensely…*fond* of you, I'd throttle you." He brushed a kiss across her cheek. "You know where I live."

And with that parting comment, he turned and walked out.

Yes, she did, Zora thought as happiness bloomed in her giddy heart once more. She knew where he lived…and she already had her toothbrush. Which seemed particularly fortuitous— she'd need to brush after she ate her humble pie.

HE'D APOLOGIZED. He'd admitted fault. He'd put the ball back into her court and he was patiently waiting for an apology.

One he was beginning to suspect he wasn't going to get. Tate knew beyond a shadow of a doubt that her conference was over. He'd factored tying up loose ends, packing up to leave, her drive home, unpacking, dinner and a lengthy shower into account…and she still hadn't shown up. He calmly channel surfed when in truth a hideous form of panic and dread had twisted his guts into knots and the idea that he was going to have to beg on top of everything else had made his palms sweat and a twitch begin near his left eye.

Oh, well, he thought, resigned. He'd beg if he must. He'd do whatever, so long as he didn't lose her. Tate reminded himself that she'd been hurt before, that she wasn't accustomed to dealing with men who told the truth. She'd need a little time to come to terms with the fact that she'd flown off the handle—had been wrong—but eventually, she'd come around.

She had to, dammit. He could make her, of course, but it wouldn't be nearly as gratifying. He'd owned up to his mistake. She should be man enough to own up to hers. The thought drew a reluctant laugh, one that, thankfully, was interrupted by the sound of his doorbell.

Though it nearly killed him, Tate took his time making his way to the door. Yes, he'd been dawdling all day, waiting for this very moment, but he had too much pride to let her know that. He smiled and opened the door. His heart lurched when he saw her and some of the tension that had been steadily tightening every vertebrae in his back lessened.

She smiled and, though he knew she didn't want him to notice the rapid pulse beating at the base of her throat, or the fact that she'd chewed her lipstick off on the way over here, Tate noted them all the same. She was endearingly—adorably—nervous.

He watched her pull in a shallow breath. "Are you going to make me apologize out here, or are you going to let me in?"

Tate grinned, belatedly stepped back and made way for her to come inside. "I'd rather you apologize naked," he told her. "But I doubt that's what you had in mind."

"In time," she said with a secret smile that instantly made his dick take notice. She strolled into his living room and took a seat on the couch. "I thought we should talk first."

Tate dropped down on the other end. "You mean you want to apologize first fully clothed, then get naked?"

A smile caught the corner of her mouth. "You're really enjoying this, aren't you?"

Tate shifted. "Hey, you got your pound of flesh—your apology—in front of a room full of people. I don't think that it's too much to ask that your apology involve a little striptease."

She considered him for a moment. Those green eyes twinkled with sexy humor, with the martial glint of challenge. She finally pulled a lazy shrug. "Fine. I don't mind…so long as you're getting naked with me."

Ordinarily Tate would have jumped at the chance, but a little devil told him that he should play hard to get. "I don't think that's a good idea. I like the idea of you being naked and humble and me being fully clothed and vindicated." Besides, he wanted to be able to fully absorb his moment of glory, and if he were naked with her he might get sidetracked.

She quirked a brow. "Scared, eh?"

She was goading him, the she-devil, Tate thought as his let's-rumble nerve issued a howl. "I'm not afraid of anything."

"Prove it. Strip with me."

"Fine," he relented. "It's not going to change anything."

Zora stood, moved around in front of him and calmly began to unbutton her blouse. Creamy skin, a V of cleavage, soft belly.

Tate swallowed, shifted as every bit of blood raced from his vital organs and hurried to his lower extremities.

She pulled another cool shrug, and the garment fell to the floor. "I'm sorry," she said, her voice oddly thick.

"For what?"

"Take off your shirt and I'll tell you."

Tate grinned, loosed the top couple of buttons and pulled his shirt off over his head. Her gaze darkened, slid over his chest and he resisted the impulsive urge to preen, to stand up and go to her. She was doing it on purpose, trying to sidetrack him. And, damn her, it was working.

Her fingers moved to her waist, smoothly unfastened her pants, then with an exaggerated slowness that made his lids droop under the weight of desire, she slid them with painstaking efficiency down her legs. Her panties were pink and lacy— like her bra—and rode high on her curvy hips. Tate blinked drunkenly, felt his dick jerk hard behind his zipper. What were they talking about again? Fault? Blame? Jeez, God, who cared? She was perfect and beautiful, his diabolical princess. Being right and vindicated was overrated. He just wanted her.

Tate stood and shucked his pants and briefs, stalked toward her.

"You win, princess," he said again, then swiftly lowered his mouth to hers. He tasted relief in her sigh, desire and something else, something he'd never sampled before.

Zora drew back, and her soft gaze tangled with his. "The only thing I want to win is you, Tate. I'm sorry I jumped to the wrong conclusion, that I didn't give you the benefit of the doubt, or even a chance to explain. It's just…I'm *immensely fond* of you, and the idea that I might have been wrong about you made me—" She struggled, growled low in her throat, seemingly at a loss for words. But it didn't matter, because he understood. She stopped trying to put her thoughts into words, leaned up and kissed him once more.

"I'm immensely fond of you as well," he told her, popping the snap on her bra. Her breasts gently tumbled free, forcing a shuddering breath from his lungs. His throat tightened with emotion. "Actually, that's a lie."

She stilled and drew back. "What?"

Tate cupped her jaw. "It's a lie. I'm not just immensely fond of you—I'm in love with you." He'd never said those words before, but they'd never been truer. He searched her gaze, watched her expression soften with emotion and awe.

"Oh, Tate," she breathed quietly. "I'm in love with you, too."

He let go the breath he'd been holding, felt a smile move across his lips. "I bet I love you more."

She laughed delightedly. "Are you sure you

want to do that? The last time we bet anything you lost."

Now that depended on your perspective, Tate thought as he found that lush mouth with his once more. From where he stood, they were both winners.

Epilogue

Six months later…

"JESUS," TATE GROWLED into Zora's ear as they danced at their reception. The last true bachelor had tied the knot with the Chicks-In-Charge chief and he couldn't be happier. Neither could the world, for that matter. To their surprise, the story of their engagement and subsequent wedding had been carried by every major network. "We've got to separate them before there's bloodshed."

Zora looked up, those pale green eyes shrewdly assessing him. She sighed, mildly exasperated, apparently at his ignorant male mentality. "For someone to be so smart, you can be pretty thick."

He grinned wryly. "Is that any way to talk to your new husband?" Her husband. He couldn't believe it. Still couldn't wrap his mind around the fact that he'd found the perfect woman and had managed to attach her to him permanently.

"Tate," she sighed patiently. Her gaze drifted to where Frankie and Ross stood, exchanging barbs over the groom's table. "Frankie and Ross are no different from how we were when we first met. You could cut the sexual tension with a knife."

He snorted, anchored her more closely to his side. "Yeah. After you pulled it out of his back. Why's she got it in for him so badly? What's he ever done?" Honestly, it didn't make any sense. His wife was convinced that there was more to it than animosity, that a healthy attraction perpetuated the continuous flow of venom between the two—she was undoubtedly right, Tate thought. She usually was, after all. But he wasn't quite so sure.

Zora's hands drifted distractingly over his back, inadvertently causing gooseflesh to slip up his spine. "He tried to hijack the reception, which was her territory, remember?"

"He was trying to be a good friend," Tate countered.

"Yes. To you," she said drolly. "However, I wasn't interested in having our reception at Hooters."

Tate chuckled fondly, remembering. "That was a joke. I wouldn't have let him do it."

Her hands drifted farther south and to his instant astonishment and arousal, she copped a feel. "I know," she sighed. "You have better taste. After all," she teased, "you married me. When can we leave?"

"I say now," he growled, nipping at her earlobe. "Let's make a quick escape."

She hesitated. "Wouldn't that be rude?"

"Who cares?" Tate countered. "This is our day."

She laughed at his blunt assessment, tilted her head up for a long, lingering kiss. Contentment welled within him, flowed through his veins as easily as the love he'd finally been able to find and accept. "Beast," she teased, her unique term of endearment.

Tate reached up and framed her face with his hands, stroked the woefully familiar slope of her cheeks. "Your beast, princess." He kissed her soundly. "And don't ever forget it."

A wicked chuckle bubbled up her throat. Her brow wrinkled in perplexed concentration. "I'm having trouble remembering." She slid him a sly glance, tugged him toward the exit. "You've got ninety seconds to remind me."

He shook his head, smiled. "Baby, I can do it in ten."

"So long as you can do it again, I don't care."

He uttered a short laugh. "That won't be a problem."

And it wasn't.

* * * * *

And the CHICKS IN CHARGE
aren't finished yet…
Don't miss seeing Frankie get Ross exactly
where she wants him,
in Blaze #172 GETTING IT GOOD!
Available next month.
Here's a preview…

Prologue

The Bet

"I'LL SEE YOUR MASSAGE and raise you a blow job."

A slow, wicked smile curved Tate Hatcher's mouth. "Confident, are you?"

Zora slid the customized fellatio chip to the center of the table and gave her husband a small enigmatic smile. *Horny* better described her current state, but let him think what he would. Confident definitely worked to her advantage.

She wasn't a great poker player and, to make matters worse, when she and Tate played Dirty Poker she always seemed to be the first player to lose focus. Her gaze skimmed over him. But who wouldn't, with a husband as sexy as hers? Her nerve endings tingled with needy anticipation and a slow steady throb commenced between her thighs. Hell, she was tempted to fold simply to get the game over with.

But she couldn't.

At least, not yet. She'd been waiting for months for a hand like this and, though he didn't know it, she intended to up the ante in an unexpected way very soon.

Tate blew out a breath and those aged-whiskey eyes shrewdly considered her. "I think you're bluffing…but on the off chance that you're not, I'm going to see your blow job—" He dropped another fellatio chip into the growing pile and lowered his voice. "And raise you a secret fantasy."

Zora arched a brow and thoughtfully tapped her cards. A secret fantasy, eh? Tate was a conservative player, didn't raise the stakes unless he was confident of the outcome, therefore one could reasonably assume that he had one helluva hand.

With effort, she suppressed a small smile. Even a helluva hand wasn't going to beat the one she currently held. The odds against him having the only hand that would beat it were too great. Out of the realm of true possibility.

In other words, she had him.

Though every nerve tingled with excited energy, Zora pretended to consider her cards once more, then let her gaze tangle with his. She cocked her head. "Why don't we make this a little more interesting?"

Tate's eyes instantly sparkled with smoky arousal. "Oh? How so?"

She leaned forward. "Let's forget Dirty Poker for the moment and talk about matchmaking between a couple of mutual friends."

The abrupt change in subject matter cleared the smoky heat from his gaze. Tate heaved a long-suffering sigh and simultaneously slouched back in his seat. "Zora, do we honestly have to have this conversation again? We shouldn't meddle. It's rude."

"It's only rude if we're wrong. And we're not. You know they're perfect for each other." An argument she'd presented for months, yet Tate still firmly refused to "meddle."

"No, I don't. I *suspect* that they would suit, however, I don't *know* and, more to the point, neither do you." He paused. "Jesus. They can't be in a room together without verbal bloodshed."

That was true, Zora had to concur. Frankie Salvaterra and Ross Hartford seemed to dislike each other simply for the pure sport of it. Though they both claimed to detest the other, they nevertheless never missed an opportunity to argue or disagree. One would think that where so much animosity existed, they would both go out of their way to avoid the other—and yet, curiously, they didn't. In fact, Zora suspected they secretly enjoyed their little battles and she further suspected that there was an underlying reason for their exaggerated aversion—intense sexual attraction. The very air around them seemed to vibrate with it, shimmery and warm. Hell, *she* could feel it.

Tate gave his head an uncertain shake and winced. "It would never work, Zora. They're like oil and water."

"Or oil and gasoline," she countered, more convinced than ever that she was right. "I think you're wrong, and if I win this hand, then you have to help me set them up."

He groaned. "That's what you meant by 'let's make it interesting'?"

She nodded. "Yep."

Tate glanced idly at his cards and something about that careless regard made her inexplicably nervous. "And what do I get if I win?"

Since there was no way she could possibly lose this hand, Zora hadn't considered what she'd offer in return. But she'd indulge him. She smiled, lowered her voice and let her gaze purposefully drop to his mouth. "What do you want?"

Tate was silent for the better part of a minute, then a slow calculating grin that made the fine hairs on her arms stand on end spread across his too-handsome face. "I want you to hire Ross, let him come to work at Chicks-In-Charge."

"What?"

Tate nodded, clearly pleased with his choice.

And no wonder. As founder of Chick's-In-Charge—a national organization designed expressly for the purpose of empowering women—Zora was adamantly opposed to hiring men for any of her ventures. Sexist? Yes. But she'd been burned very badly by a former boyfriend/boss—which was how Chicks-In-Charge had gotten its start in the first place—and so far the concept had worked very well for her. She provided a completely testosterone-free workplace and all of her employees loved it.

Zora frowned thoughtfully. Particularly Frankie, who'd been scorched pretty badly by her father. "You know I can't do that," Zora finally said, mildly irritated. Hell, she'd compromised her principles enough by getting married. *Hire a man?* No way. "Besides, he has a job. He wouldn't take it."

"Oh, I can guarantee that he would take it." An evil sort of glee clung to his smile. "If he wants the Maxwell account he'll take it."

Zora gasped. "Tate, that's horrible." And, yet so diabolical she found it sexy. "Hadn't you planned on giving him that account anyway?"

Smiling, he nodded. "Yeah...but he doesn't know that. Besides, it would be worth it to see you add a man to your payroll." He shifted in his seat, looked heavenward and heaved a dramatic sigh. *"God, would it ever be worth it."*

"You know I can't do that," Zora replied tightly. "Pick something else. Anything else."

"Nope. That's what I want," he insisted, to Zora's supreme irritation. He thoughtfully considered her once more and one side of his mouth kicked up in a faintly smug smile. "Guess you're not as confident as I thought you were. That, or you just don't want this bad enough."

Though she knew better than to react, the somewhat mocking taunt overrode her initial hesitation. "Oh, I'm confident, and I most definitely want this." Frankie needed someone. Desperately. And Zora simply knew—*knew*—that Ross was the man for her. Besides, there was simply no way Tate could beat her hand. The odds were too great against it. Still, if hell froze over and she did lose this hand, then it would be better to have set a few conditions and parameters. "Temporary employment?"

"Define 'temporary.'"

"A week."

Tate laughed. "Not long enough. A month."

"Two weeks," Zora countered.

He nodded succinctly. "Done. What have you got?"

Now, for the moment of truth. Zora grinned and carefully spread her hand down on the table. "I've got a straight flush, baby. Read 'em and weep." She threw her head back and a giddy burst of triumphant laughter bubbled up her throat.

Tate hummed under his breath and his head bobbed a single nod of agreement. "That is a good hand," he conceded lightly. "But mine's better—"

Zora's gleeful chortling came to an abrupt halt and the smile slid from her face. *"What?"*

"Because I've got a *royal* flush." Tate laid his cards down on the table.

Stunned, Zora shook her head. Dread curdled in her stomach. "No— But you can't— I-It's not possible."

He smiled. "Oh, but it is." He cheerfully slid the pot from the middle of the table. "So, what do I want first?" Tate pondered aloud with the exaggerated air of a child who'd just been told Christmas had come early this year. "Do I want a massage? A blow job? A secret fantasy?" His eyes twinkled with evil humor. "Or do I want you to call Ross *right now* and offer him a job?" He pretended to think about it for a couple of seconds, then nodded dramatically. "Yeah. That's what I want. I want you to call Ross. Right now." Then to Zora's immense irritation, he howled with laughter.

"If you're going to have to blackmail him into

taking the position shouldn't I wait until we can both talk to him?"

Still laughing, Tate shook his head. "No."

A frustrated growl vibrated the back of Zora's throat. "Dammit, Tate, I don't even know what I'm going to hire him to do, for pity's sake."

God, what *was* she going to hire him to do? Zora wondered with mounting alarm. There were no current openings, she was fully staffed at *CHiC*, her Web-based e-zine, which had just made its debut in a glossy format. Furthermore, since it looked like she would definitely have to add Ross to the payroll—albeit only for two weeks—she should definitely make the most of them by putting Ross and Frankie in close proximity. Which would be next to impossible because Frankie— *CHiC*'s resident sex-pert, the Carnal Contessa— would be on tour promoting the new glossy format the magazine had recently adopted.

Zora paused as a flush of inspiration suddenly lessened the panic crowding her brain. Wait a minute. This could actually work to her advantage. *What if…* A slow smile worked its way across her lips. *Oh, God. That was perfect.* Tate had not specified in what capacity she had to hire Ross, just simply that she must.

Tate's laughter trailed off and ended with a deep satisfied sigh. He glanced at her, then frowned. "Why are you smiling?" he asked warily. "I won. I'm the one who's smiling. Not you. You're not supposed to smile. You're supposed to worry and fret and eat humble pie. This is supposed to be a character lesson, a crash course in the benefit of humility."

Zora grinned. "Whatever."

"Whatever? What do you mean whatever?" His eyes narrowed. "Just what exactly have you got up your sleeve?"

"You'll see," Zora replied mysteriously. "Right now, however, I believe I have a few plans to make."

Silhouette

Desire

Don't miss the next story in

Dixie Browning's
new miniseries

DIVAS WHO DISH

These three friends can dish it out, but can they take it?

HER MAN UPSTAIRS
Available February 2005
(Silhouette Desire #1634)

Sparks flew when laid-back carpenter Cole Stevens
met his beautiful and feisty new boss, Marty Owens.
She was instantly attracted to Cole, but knew that the
higher she flew the harder she'd fall. Could her heart
handle falling for the man upstairs?

Available at your favorite retail outlet.

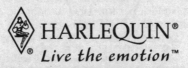